HER SILENT NIGHT

A MARTINA MONROE CHRISTMAS THRILLER

H.K. CHRISTIE

This is a work of fiction. Names, characters, businesses, places, events and incidents are either the products of the author's imagination or used in a fictitious manner. Any resemblance to actual persons, living or dead, or actual events is purely coincidental.

Copyright © 2025 by H.K. Christie

Cover design by Odile Stamanne

All rights reserved.

No part of this book may be reproduced in any form or by any electronic or mechanical means, including information storage and retrieval systems, without written permission from the publisher, except for the use of brief quotations in a book review.

If you would like to use material from this book, prior written permission must be obtained by contacting the publisher at:

www.authorhkchristie.com

First edition: September 2025

ISBN: 978-1-953268-36-5

191125

For all the kids who spent Christmas break huddled under blankets, wide-eyed in the glow of the TV, daring themselves to watch just one more scary movie.

1

HIM

The man's head hit the floor with a dull, wet thud. His body twitched once and then went still. I stood over him, breath ragged, the fireplace poker slick in my gloved hand. Blood pooled beneath his temple and spread onto the hardwood floor. I hadn't wanted things to get messy, but some things and some people deserved the mess.

I dragged his body across the living room, unfortunately leaving long, red smears along the way. I'd have to be quick with the cleanup, but I was prepared. I'd already planned to wipe everything down before I left. I'd planned for every detail, because everything had to be perfect. My message had to be clear.

From my kit, I grabbed the clear packing tape and wrapped it around his head to keep the blood contained. Less mess was better. After wiping up the surrounding mess, I turned to the Santa suit I had laid out on the couch. It was a high-end deep burgundy velvet, not the cheap kind you'd find at Walmart or Target. It was special ordered.

I knelt beside the man and removed his jacket, then tugged off his slacks, stripping him down to his undergarments. He was heavier than I had expected. His limbs flopped with dead weight as I slid the red pants over his legs and then pulled the jacket on over his torso, buttoning it neatly. I tugged the cap over his graying hair, and finally, the boots. They were shiny and black with gold buckles that glinted under the living room lights.

He was dressed for the holidays, like he'd done in the past. He probably didn't think I knew about that. But I did. Of course I did. My only regret was that I didn't get to tell him why this was his fate. Maybe he knew someone would come for him, eventually. Karma was like that.

The scene was nearly perfect. A Christmas tree stood beside the fireplace, its branches heavy with lights and ornaments. Stockings were hung with care. Flameless candles lined the mantel and side tables.

Once he was dressed, I went around to each of the candles and flicked them on. Marvelous little things they were. Flickering like real flames, their light danced across the walls. As I stared down at the grisly picture, I thought about what he'd done. Those actions had dire consequences. Heartbreaking, life-shattering consequences.

It was time they paid for their sins. Time for the world to understand what they'd done. Time to stop it, once and for all.

I lifted the man's shoulders and shoved him. The chimney was tight, but not impossible. It was trickier than I'd expected. His limbs caught on the brick and his shoulders resisted the angle. Still, I continued. Shoving. Forcing. Until he was wedged inside.

All you could see now were the black, shining boots and the edges of red velvet pants brushing the hearthstone. I stepped back and studied my work. It was a symbol. But more than that, it was a reckoning.

At the hearth, I struck a match. The dry pine kindling at the bottom snapped to life quickly, flames crackling. Heat shot upward in sharp waves. I watched for a moment, letting the scent of smoke and scorched cotton fill the room. It was thick and bitter, the way Christmas *never* should be.

After a moment, I turned away and moved toward the mantel, to the first stocking, and slipped a red envelope inside.

Before I began the cleanup, I let my gaze drift back to the fire. The flames were climbing. Each moment, they curled higher as they raced up the chimney toward the body. The image stayed in my mind as I scrubbed every surface, wiping away every trace of myself. Even with gloves and a hat, you could never be too careful. With a nod, I stepped out into the chilly early hours of the dark December morning, my heartbeat steady and my soul satisfied. *For now*.

2

DETECTIVE KATE MADDOX

The body was still wedged in the chimney when I arrived. The details dispatch provided were foggy, but clear enough to know I was walking into a crime scene unlike any I'd seen before.

I stepped out of the car and zipped up my jacket against the Bay Area chill. It was midmorning, and the sun hid behind a thick layer of low, gray clouds. The rain had tapered to a mist, just enough to slick the pavement and give the air that familiar December dampness.

The Victorian-style house sat on a quiet street in Oakland, its fresh coat of paint still gleaming faintly despite the gloom. A bright "For Sale" sign swayed gently on its post. Everything about it screamed new beginnings, except the body inside.

As I climbed the wooden steps to the front door, drops of water slipped from the edge of the roof onto my shoulders. I held up my badge to the uniform posted out front. "Detective Maddox, Homicide."

The patrol officer, young, probably still shaking off academy jitters, stepped aside quickly. "They're waiting for you inside."

Before ducking under the yellow crime scene tape, I paused. "Who's in there?"

"Officer Granger, the M.E., and a few techs."

"Who called it in?"

"The gardener. This morning, he noticed smoke coming from the chimney and called the homeowner. The house was supposed to be empty. It had been staged weeks ago for showing prospective buyers. The owner figured it was squatters or vandals." He shifted his stance. "When the responding officer got here, the front door was unlocked. He stepped inside, and that's when he found the body."

"Who was the responding officer?"

As if on cue, Officer Ogden approached, nodding in greeting. We'd worked together before, enough to skip the usual pleasantries. "You found him?"

He let out a slow breath. "Yeah. It's... creepy. Brace yourself."

After ten years in homicide, I'd learned there's always something worse waiting behind the next door. Just when you think you've seen it all, some new kind of awful showed its face. Ogden led me through the house.

The interior was crisp and impersonal aside from the Christmas decor. It was cold, the house's heating system was likely off. New furniture filled the rooms, throw pillows fluffed, a cozy blanket folded over the arm of a couch that had never been used. On the mantel above the fireplace, battery-operated candles flickered. Four red stockings hung from silver hooks. And below it was the reason I was there.

Two charred boots, with exposed flesh, dangled from the fireplace. The legs were dressed in what looked like blackened velvet pants, soot-streaked and stiff. Based on the angle, the body was wedged deep and bent at a grotesquely unnatural slant. Whoever had stuffed him in there hadn't done it gently. I could only hope the victim had already been dead.

Dr. Lang, the medical examiner, was squatting near the hearth, a flashlight tilted upward to illuminate the inside of the chimney. She turned toward me and stood up. "Hi, Kate," she said as I approached. "It's a doozy today."

I exhaled slowly, eyes fixed on the boots. "I can see that. How on Earth could a body get shoved in there?"

"If it were a newer home, it would be darn near impossible. But in an old Victorian like this one, the fireplace opening is much wider. It's difficult to see from your viewpoint, but my guess is it's about 42 inches wide at the bottom and narrows toward the top."

The killer had to have known that. Had they staked out the place ahead of time? They must have seen that the house was for sale, vacant and, therefore, a prime location for their horrific crime. "Learn something new every day."

She smirked. "Indeed. We're about to remove the body. They've already vacuumed for evidence and documented everything."

She gave a quick update to the two crime scene techs standing by. We exchanged a solemn nod before they stepped forward with portable scaffolding, already assembled to reach up into the chimney's firebox.

I took a step back, my shoes squeaking slightly on the polished hardwood. The interior of the house was eerily quiet, no hum of heat, no ticking clock, no sign of life beyond the crime scene itself.

The techs began loosening the bricks, one at a time. The scrape of metal tools against mortar echoed faintly through the air. Damp ash floated up with every shift, carrying with it the sharp scent of soot and scorched creosote. The body resisted. It was wedged in tight.

It took nearly fifteen minutes of delicate work before the torso finally slipped free, landing on the plastic tarp below with a dull thump, like a sack of laundry. The smell hit instantly. Burnt fabric. Singed hair. Cooked flesh. Even after a decade in homicide, that particular mix still made my stomach clench.

It was unclear what the man once looked like, as his face had been wrapped in tape distorting his features. His Santa suit wasn't some cheap party-store knockoff, it was high end. Rich red velvet, thick fur trim, now streaked with soot and blistered at the sleeves. The velvet pants were scorched near the cuffs, blackened where the flames had kicked upward from the fire. His boots were worse and melted slightly at the soles, the leather cracked and singed from direct heat.

Dr. Lang crouched beside the body and pulled on a fresh pair of gloves.

I scanned the room. The rest of the space was pristine. No signs of a struggle. "Do we have an ID?"

"I'll check his pockets," Dr. Lang said and then began a methodical pat-down. Jacket pockets were empty. The pants had no pockets at all. She checked again just to be sure, then looked up and shook her head. "No wallet. No phone. No keys. No identification."

"So all we know is we have a dead Santa."

She peeled back the velvet jacket and lifted the shirt beneath. "No tags on the suit either."

"Could've been custom."

"Or," Ogden said, stepping in, "whoever dressed him didn't want him identified."

"Or he dressed himself for an event and was taken. If he had, he likely didn't expect to die in it."

Maybe he was a mall Santa. Or someone hired for a holiday party or a charity event. "What about the shoes?"

Dr. Lang removed each boot carefully. "Nothing inside," and she flipped them over. "Any identifiers were cooked."

She stood and wiped her gloves down with a sterile cloth.

"No ID. No phone. No wallet. No name," she said. "Our first Santa Doe."

She moved to the head, examining the scalp and face, but didn't remove the tape. "Looks like blunt force trauma on the right side before he was shoved in."

"Do you think he was alive when it happened?" I asked.

Dr. Lang leaned in, inspecting his eyes, then his nose and mouth through the clear tape that had been hastily applied. "Based on the tape and head wound, not likely," she said. "But once I do the autopsy, we'll be able to determine if he was breathing when he was put in there and set on fire."

One of the techs approached, holding up a clear evidence bag. "Found this inside one of the stockings."

He handed it to me. Inside was a vintage-style Christmas card. A delicate watercolor of a snow-covered cottage, a sleigh in the distance, trees painted soft and pale.

The inside read:

He wore the suit for fun. They wore the scars.
    Merry Christmas.

In the lower corner, there was a small, hand-drawn snowflake.

Dr. Lang leaned in to read it. "What do you think it means?"

I shook my head slowly. "I'm not sure. At this point, anything's possible."

A buzz in my jacket alerted me. Pulling out my phone, I read the text message from Natalie, a local crime reporter and friend. She was on her way to the scene. I thought, *That was fast.* The thoughts that followed were, *the media is going to love this one.*

3

MARTINA

Tightening the scarf around my neck, I grabbed the box of cookies I'd spent several hours baking with my mom. She called it a trial run for the big day, the big day being Christmas, when Zoey and her new husband would be home, and Selena would come over along with Hirsch and Vincent's families. Everyone would be gathered around the Christmas tree, and Mom said she wanted to make sure we had a good sampling of treats.

She'd twisted my arm into joining her, insisting it would be a new tradition for our family. Despite my initial reluctance, I'd had fun and looked forward to when Zoey and Selena could join us. Zoey had always loved being in the kitchen with my mom. And truthfully, I liked sampling the finished product. But I was never the type to bake cookies and sing Christmas carols.

Still, I'd decided this year would be different. We were going to have a joy-filled Christmas without any investigations or chasing bad guys. Peace, joy, and love would be all around.

As I approached the porch, I veered toward the mailbox and grabbed the stack of mail before heading inside. The moment I opened the door, I laughed. Barney was right there to greet me.

"Okay, okay! Hi, Barney! Oh, I missed you too," I said, smiling as he danced around my legs. I knelt down, balancing one box of cookies, my keys, and the mail. Barney's excitement quickly turned into curious sniffing at the cookie box. "Alright, alright, let me get inside first."

With a quick kick, I shut the door behind me and latched the lock. Barney let out a delighted yelp and began zooming down the hall and around the living room, knocking over one of the gifts under the Christmas tree. Charlie, my handsome husband, peeked around the corner and grinned.

"Oh, is Mommy home, Barney? I see why you're so excited. I am too!"

Barney paused to beg for scratches, then resumed his mad dash through the house. I waved. "I've brought cookies."

Charlie raised an eyebrow. "What did *you* make?"

"Well, I was pretty much my mom's sous chef," I said, setting the box on the dining table, along with the mail.

"Chocolate chip with red and green M&M's, peanut butter cookies with chocolate kisses, snickerdoodles, and sugar cookies with frosting. I'll have you know, I added the sprinkles."

Charlie grinned from ear to ear. "You added the sprinkles? Zoey's going to be very jealous."

"Mom says this is just a practice bake off. With two weeks until Christmas, she plans to bake fresh batches once we decide which ones are the winners."

"No brownies?"

"Apparently those are for another day."

Charlie walked over, wrapping his arms around me. I leaned into him and gave him a warm kiss. He mumbled, "It's so nice to have you home."

"It is, isn't it?" It wasn't like me to take two weeks off of work in December, but it had been quite a year. I think we could all use a bit of a break, one filled with tinsel, twinkle lights, and cookies. And, if Charlie had his way, brownies too.

After our embrace, Charlie went straight for the box of cookies. I swear, he was just like Barney that way. I chuckled and picked up the stack of mail. On top was an envelope. It was bright red with no return address. Just my name written in neat block letters:

MARTINA MONROE.

I furrowed my brow, but continued sorting through the rest of the mail. Bills, catalogues, and a card from the vet. Nothing else interesting. Before I could investigate the strange envelope further, Charlie called out from the kitchen, his mouth full, "These snickerdoodles are excellent."

"I agree," I said, setting the mail aside. "Mom made me sample at least a bite of each one. Now I'm going to have to go for a run."

"Oh, nonsense," he said, popping another cookie into his mouth. "You look fantastic. A few cookies around the holidays aren't going to change that."

"But sugar..." I warned playfully. "You've got to even out your blood sugar with exercise. I certainly don't want diabetes."

He gave me a look, the same one he always gave me when I got too uptight about things.

Since I'd been with Charlie, I'd loosened up a little. My rigid eating habits and strict exercise routines had softened a little. Charlie was a gifted cook, just like my mom. And yes, I'd gained a few pounds, but that wasn't what worried me. I was at the age where I had to be careful. I wanted a long and healthy life. But he was right; a few cookies around the holidays, or dessert once or even twice a week, wasn't going to hurt.

Charlie had brought so much joy into my life—like

Christmas cheer, warmth, laughter, and a daughter. Selena had become like one of my own, and she was one of the top private investigators at my firm. He'd welcomed Zoey as if she were his, too. My darling daughter, now in her third year of veterinary school in Oregon. I was so proud of her. Both of my daughters were amazing women. And now, I had a son-in-law, Henry.

There was a time when things weren't so bright and cheerful.

When Zoey was little, it had been just the two of us. After her father, Jared, died, I didn't know how I'd go on. We had Stavros. He was my boss back then, but also like an uncle. My mother and I had been estranged. So had I been with my brothers. The holidays were a time I used to dread. But everything had changed.

I'd found friends, true friends. Hirsch and his wife, Kim. My mother had come back into my life, and now I couldn't imagine living without her. My brother had gotten clean, married, and even had a baby. And of course, there was Selena. And Charlie. And Barney, our little rescue pup. A fluffball full of love who had completely stolen our hearts.

I glanced over at him now, wrestling his new plush reindeer. He loved his toys, especially at Christmastime. No one could resist buying him a new one, and he never tired of them. I smiled. I'd grown softer over the years, yes, but maybe that wasn't such a bad thing.

Charlie's voice broke into my thoughts. "Who's this from?"

My gaze returned to the red envelope. "I don't know. It was just in the mailbox, with the rest of the mail."

"There's no address, like someone dropped it off. Maybe it's from one of the neighbors?"

"Could be," I said, picking it up again. I carefully opened the flap. Inside was a vintage Christmas card, illustrated with a classic Santa Claus carrying a sack over his shoulder, standing beside a fireplace and a glittering tree with stockings hung above the hearth. The image was charming. Nostalgic. But when I opened the card, a chill ran down my spine.

The pre-printed message said:

Wishing you a joy filled holiday season

Below that, in blocky, handwritten letters, someone had scrawled:

He wore the suit for fun. They wore the scars. You can make them see.
 Merry Christmas

In the bottom corner was a small, hand-drawn snowflake. My stomach twisted.

I could feel Charlie's eyes on me. "What is it?"

"It's... strange," I said, staring at the words. "It doesn't say who it's from. Just this weird message."

"Weird how?" he asked.

I turned the card so he could read it for himself. He took a moment, then met my gaze. "That is weird."

I nodded slowly and set the card down on the table beside the cookies. I wasn't sure what to make of it. But there was something very unsettling about it.

"Are you worried?"

I hesitated. "No... maybe. I don't know." I rubbed the back of my neck. "Did you make any coffee?"

Coffee always helped me think clearly. For some people, it made them jittery and unfocused, but for me, it did the opposite. It was my last real vice, the one I still allowed myself. Something about the warmth, the smell, and the ritual. It grounded me.

"I can make some."

"That would be great. Thanks." I gave him a small smile. Charlie really was the best. Absentmindedly, I grabbed another cookie from the box. That was the real reason I didn't keep sweets in the house very often. I liked them. I liked cookies. I liked ice cream. I liked curling up on the couch with Charlie and eating popcorn while we watched a movie together.

We used to do that when Zoey was little, our Friday movie night tradition. Pizza, soda, candy, ice cream—whatever she wanted, I gave in. But the truth was, it wasn't just for her. It was for me too. And I think she always knew that. I smiled at the memory, just as Charlie returned with two steaming mugs of coffee.

"Hey," he said, handing me one, "did you read the paper today?"

"No. Why?"

"Grisly crime."

"Grisly crime?" I echoed, my brow furrowing.

He nodded, settling into the chair across from me. "Apparently, a guy dressed as Santa was shoved up a chimney. He's dead."

I froze, the mug halfway to my lips. "That's... terrible."

"Yeah. Surprised you didn't hear about it."

"When did it happen?"

"Yesterday, I think. It's in today's Bay Insider."

"Interesting," I said, setting the coffee down. I reached for my phone, still tasting cinnamon and sugar from the snickerdoodle as I typed in the search. Within seconds, the headline appeared at the top of the screen. ***CHIMNEY DEATH RECALLS INFAMOUS HOLIDAY HORRORS.*** My stomach clenched. I clicked the link, and I started to read.

∼

CHIMNEY DEATH RECALLS INFAMOUS HOLIDAY HORRORS

By Natalie Sloane – The Bay Insider

OAKLAND, Calif. — A man dressed in a Santa suit was found dead inside a chimney Thursday morning, in what investigators have confirmed is being treated as a homicide.

"This was definitely not accidental," Detective Kate Maddox told The Bay Insider. While she declined to provide further details, the unusual nature of the crime has already sparked comparisons to one of the most infamous and unsettling holiday scenes in pop culture: the dark tale told by Phoebe Cates's character in the 1984 film "Gremlins."

In the film, Cates's character recounts a chilling Christmas memory—how her father, dressed as Santa, attempted to surprise his family by coming down the chimney. He never made it out. Days later, his body was discovered. A horrifying twist wrapped in holiday cheer.

While that particular story was fiction, history has proven the concept isn't unique. The results of my search on the scenario were disturbing. Most notable was the story of a 19-year-old man who died in Huron, Calif. in 2015. The young man had tried to enter a home, in order to burglarize it, through the chimney. But the homeowner, unaware of the intruder's presence, lit the fireplace. Neighbors later reported hearing screams. By the time responders got to him, he was dead.

As gruesome as this incident was, it isn't as rare as you would like to think. There have been more than a few Santa-types who died trying to come down the chimney. But this most recent case, the one here in Oakland, feels different. The scene was staged, the costume intentional, the symbolism unmistakable. This wasn't an accident, or a botched burglary. It was deliberate. Calculated. The holiday season, for all its joy, has a darker history than most realize. And someone out there may be using that darkness to send a message.

I set down my phone and looked over at Charlie, my expression tight. "Well," I said, "that doesn't exactly spell holiday cheer." My thoughts drifted back to the red envelope with the odd holiday greeting, and an uneasiness settled in.

"Nope," he said, shaking his head. "Aren't you glad you're not working a case?"

"I am."

Charlie's mouth twitched into a grim sort of smile. In a dry, deadpan voice, he muttered, "Ho ho ho."

4

HIM

I stretched my arms overhead and glanced down the hallway. None of my neighbors were around. It wasn't unusual. It was one of the perks of the building. Most of the residents were quiet and kept to themselves. I bent down and picked up the newspaper, the paper kind. Not the glowing screen most people worshipped these days. I preferred the weight of newsprint in my hands, and the way the ink smudged my fingertips.

I carried it inside and settled on my sofa. My legs stretched out onto the coffee table. Flipping through the pages, I hunted for what I knew would be there. Not front-page material. Of course not. The city buried the stories it didn't want anyone talking about. Page six. Below the fold. And there it was: "Chimney Death Recalls Infamous Holiday Horrors," by Natalie Sloane – The Bay Insider.

The Bay Insider. One of the last publications stubborn enough to print on paper. I read every word twice. Not all the details were there, but the last line caught me. I read it again. *And again.*

The reporter had *understood* that it was a message. My lips pulled into a smile. Setting the paper down, I tore the article out with care. I laid it flat on the coffee table. Then, picking up a thick black marker, I circled her name, Natalie Sloane, in slow, deliberate strokes.

Natalie Sloane. A strong name. Bold. Certain. The kind of name that belonged to someone who didn't look away and mind their own business. I stood and carried the clipping to my corkboard. The pushpin slid in with a satisfying snap, the article landing beside the one about the 2005 fire, and the list of names I still had left to visit.

Natalie's listening, I thought. Somebody's listening. It wasn't the cops. They'd failed. It wasn't the courts. They'd failed too. And the caseworkers? Long gone.

A reporter could make people see. I hadn't considered that option for broadcasting to the world. I'd already sent a message to someone else. Someone whose name had crossed the newspaper pages more than a few times, dragging criminals into the light, exposing corrupt cops, politicians, and organized crime. A woman fearless in taking down predators. A woman who gave victims a voice. *Martina Monroe.* A mother. A private investigator. A cold case investigator. But I could see there was another person to help with the cause.

Martina Monroe and Natalie Sloane would help people see the truth. They would bring justice to those who deserved it. But until they understood the cause, I'd have to send another message. And another. Until it was crystal clear what I needed them to do. What I needed them to expose. And who needed to pay.

5

DETECTIVE KATE MADDOX

Staring at the crime scene photos from the chimney murder, I tried to make sense of it. Why would somebody do that? Could it be someone who knew about other instances of chimney deaths, like Natalie had? Was it symbolic? Perhaps the killer was just a sadistic individual who hated Christmas. But who hates Christmas that much? Enough to murder someone, dress them in a Santa suit, and then shove them up a chimney? Until we had an ID on the body, we had no idea of the motive. Once we had a name, we could learn everything about the victim and hopefully that would lead to his killer.

I'd seen a lot of things in my day, but this... this took the tinsel right off the Christmas tree.

Not that I'd ever been all that into Christmas myself, or any holiday, really. Growing up without parents, there wasn't much to be jolly about. Sure, I had a few kind foster parents along the way, but it didn't make up for losing my mom and dad. Looking back, I admit, I wasn't the easiest child, which probably made me a little harder to love. Maybe the holidays could have been filled with cheer if I'd tried a little. But it wasn't like I had chosen to be abandoned by my parents and shoved into the system. I guess it wasn't their choice either, since they'd been killed in a car accident when I was seven. My only relative was my grandmother on my mom's side, but she was in a care facility and couldn't take care of me. There was nobody else.

I did remember my last Christmas with my parents. Although I wondered if those were real memories, or just ones I wished were true. I read somewhere that every time we recall a memory, it changes. So who knew what was real and what wasn't? But in my mind, I could still see the Christmas tree lit up in the corner, twinkling against the shiny wrapping paper of a giant box with a big red bow on top. Next to it, leaning against the wall, was a pink Huffy bike. I'd screamed so loud my mother had covered her ears with her hands. I don't think I've ever felt that kind of excitement since. Inside the box was a Barbie Dream house.

I shook my head at the memory. That dream house, like the idea of any dream home, shattered shortly after. My parents died just a few weeks later. The roads were slick from the recent rains, when my parents drove the winding hills on their way home from a friend's house in Berkeley. Another driver, fresh from their own party, blew through a stop sign and hit them, causing them to lose control.

Maybe that was why I'd kept my distance from the holiday ever since, and why I was always the one to volunteer to be on call during the season. Most of the other detectives had families or people to celebrate with.

Last Christmas, Natalie and I met at a bar on Christmas Eve. We called it the meeting of the Christmas Orphan Club. Her parents were gone too, and she didn't have any family. It was something that bonded us despite our ten-year age difference.

My phone vibrated on my desk, yanking me out of my memories. "Maddox."

The voice on the other end of the line was brisk. "Hey, it's Jeff. We got an ID on the victim from the chimney murder. It is sixty-seven-year-old Garrett Slade."

That was fast. "How did you make the ID?"

"His fingerprints are in the system. He was registered as a foster parent up until about ten years ago."

My stomach tightened. "Really?" I kept my tone neutral, but my fingers curled into my palm. From my experience, a former foster parent could have dozens of people who may want to hurt them.

Glancing at the clock in the corner of my computer monitor, I didn't have much time before Child Protective Services would be closing for the day. I needed to contact the agency's law enforcement liaison and request all his records. His licensing application, home study reports, complaint and investigation history, and the names of all foster children placed with him. If I couldn't put in the request this afternoon, I'd have to wait until Monday. "Did you find any other prints at the scene?"

Jeff was the lead crime scene tech and we'd worked together for the better part of a decade. He was solid, and fast. He obviously understood the urgency on the case. "No hits. The place was wiped clean."

"Hairs? Fibers?"

"We're still processing the clothes, but my guess our killer thought this out, and knew how to clean up a scene."

Great. That wasn't going to make my job any easier. "Thanks, Jeff."

"Sure thing. I'll let you know if we find anything else."

With the call ended, I pulled up the number for CPS but as I was about to dial, I received another call. "Maddox."

Dr. Lang said, "The preliminary tox report is back, and the autopsy's done."

"I'll be right over." I preferred to see the bodies, as opposed to just hear about the findings, so I shoved my phone into my pocket and headed down to the autopsy suite. After gowning up, I buzzed in, and the heavy metal door shut behind me. The scent hit first. It was sterile and metallic, with that faint undercurrent of something sweet and rotten that clung to the back of your throat no matter how many times you'd experienced it.

Dr. Lang, a woman in her mid-forties, stood beside the steel table, gloved hands resting lightly on the edge, her eyes already on me. "Afternoon, Kate."

"Hey. What did you find in the tox screen?"

"The initial panel showed our victim full of flunitrazepam. He was drugged."

Flunitrazepam was the generic name for Rohypnol, a powerful sedative often known as the date rape drug. "That makes sense, considering the scene," I said. My jaw clenched as I pictured it. "Whoever did this had to get him up all those stairs somehow. It would've been impossible for one person to carry a man that size without a little help. If he was still semi-conscious, the killer could've walked him up, pretending to be a friend, then once inside—" I tapped the side of my head, "—whacked him and went to work."

"It's plausible," Dr. Lang agreed. "It also explains how he was subdued enough to be undressed and then put in a Santa suit, and then shoved up a chimney. If he wasn't already dead, he would've been knocked out from the drug."

I glanced down at the sheet draped over the body. "What else did you find?"

"Well, for a sixty-seven-year-old man, he wasn't in good shape. Artery disease, bad liver. Honestly, he probably had maybe ten years left, if that. I'd guess he was a big drinker, ate a lot of junk food, and didn't take care of himself."

I shifted my weight, resisting the urge to pace. Probably

didn't take good care of his foster kids, either. "Was he dead when the killer shoved him up there?"

"There was no soot found in his lungs. He was likely dead from suffocation once the tape was placed over his nose and mouth, but he would've bled out quickly from the head wound if given the chance."

I stood staring at the victim. The sheet covered him up to his chin. His face was pudgy and gray, framed by bushy eyebrows. He didn't look kind, but then again, most people didn't look all warm and fuzzy while lying on a slab. "Did you find anything unusual?"

"Not really. My guess is he was hit on the head with a narrow heavy object, maybe a tire iron or fireplace poker, taped up, and then, I surmised based on the lack of blood on the Santa suit, redressed after the taping. Then shoved up into the chimney."

"Who even has the idea to do that?"

"I certainly wouldn't," Dr. Lang said. "I don't plot out murders on a daily basis, but if I did, that wouldn't be the first thing that popped into my mind," she said with a playful smirk.

"I hear ya. Call me if you find anything unusual."

"Will do, but it's pretty run-of-the-mill. I'll send you the report when it's done."

"Thanks."

As I exited, the words from Jeff wouldn't stop echoing in my head. Our victim was a foster parent. I wondered if he'd had any complaints filed against him because that could point straight toward a motive. Retaliation. But he hadn't been active in ten years. Would someone really wait a decade to hunt him down and kill him, right before Christmas, in such a gruesome way?

Thinking back to my own time in the system, my throat tightened. I had my share of trauma, but I'd also had copious amounts of therapy to help me get past it. If I hadn't, or if I'd been wired just a little differently, maybe it was possible I'd be seeking revenge myself. My Friday night plans were clear. I needed to learn everything I could about Garrett Slade.

After stripping off the booties and scrubs, I headed back toward my desk. My phone buzzed, and I answered. "Hey, Natalie. What's up?"

"You wanna grab dinner tonight?"

"I've got a pile of work on my desk. We just got an ID on our victim, a former foster parent."

Natalie chuckled. "So you probably have about two hundred possible suspects?"

"Depends. I need to do a full background on this guy and start contacting family and friends. I'm getting a lot of pressure to solve this one, and fast."

"You have to eat."

"True. I'll text you later, maybe around eight?"

"Cool."

With the call ended, my thoughts returned to our victim. Who was Garrett Slade, and was he targeted or some unfortunate sap who crossed paths with the wrong person?

6

DETECTIVE KATE MADDOX

After my third cup of coffee, I shook my head. I'd need to request more resources.

I'd received the records from CPS on Garrett Slade late Friday night. He and his wife had nearly seventy-five foster kids in their home during their time as foster parents. That was a lot of people to look into, and they might not even be related to the case.

To make matters worse, I couldn't find next of kin. According to his records, he had no family and no life insurance policy. He owned his home outright. He'd been retired and collecting social security for the last two years, so there weren't even any coworkers to question.

Before he retired, he'd worked at a grocery store. He'd probably been able to buy the house because he supplemented his income with foster care payments. His record was squeaky clean, shockingly so. Who has never gotten a parking ticket? He had no complaints in the fifteen years he was a foster parent. No official grievances. But that didn't mean there weren't any. If Slade was a bad man, he could have threatened the children into silence.

The home study report showed children who were well fed and clothed. So far, all this meant we had no leads, and I was shooting in the dark. I'd have my hands full trying to find dozens of former foster kids to question, and to go and talk to his neighbors to learn about his habits. Did he keep to himself? Was he friendly? Did he get many visitors? Did he and his wife really have one of the few great foster homes?

Maybe once we got his name out in the papers, people would come forward who could help us out. I called Natalie.

"What's up?"

"I was wondering if you could run a follow-up story on our victim now that we've got the name? I haven't been able to locate a next of kin. It would be good to ask the public for help in learning more about him and his last movements."

"Sure. Can it wait till Monday?"

One more day wouldn't hurt. "It can."

"You sound tired. Have you been working all weekend?"

Yes. I'd only been able to sleep a few hours on Friday and Saturday nights. My mind couldn't quit thinking about the murder and possible motives. It was very possible the fact he had been a foster parent could have nothing to do with his death. It could have been random or someone else in Slade's life who wanted revenge for some perceived crime. "Mostly. I still have a lot of work ahead of me if I'm going to solve this. I'd like to close this up in a neat little bow, like a Christmas gift."

"Yeah," Natalie said, "that would be something. Do you want any company?"

"Not today. I need to search his house with the guys, and question neighbors, see what I can find out about the victim." We had no personal effects of his. There was a BOLO out on his vehicle, but so far, nobody had found it. The only place to search, at this point, was his home.

"Okay, let me know if you want to grab dinner."

"I'll talk to you later."

Natalie always wanted to tag along during investigations, but she was a reporter and I was a detective. On more than one occasion, I'd asked her why she didn't just go into law enforcement herself. She said she was too much of a rebel and didn't like all the rules, but Nat respected my boundaries, which is why I always gave her the inside scoop when I could.

∽

THIRTY MINUTES LATER, I arrived in the vic's neighborhood. Like many homes in the area, Slade's house was small, but cared-for. The siding was clean, paint in good shape. I wouldn't have expected that from a man who didn't take care of himself physically, but apparently he took pride in his home.

I glanced around the neighborhood. There were houses on either side, one directly across the street. Curtains in the front window were drawn slightly back, as though someone had peeked out recently. I stepped closer and looked inside. The living room wasn't spotless, but it wasn't a disaster either, just a little clutter.

The front door was locked. No car in the driveway. That meant he likely hadn't been abducted from his residence. I wandered around to the side of the house. Peering over the fence, I saw a small yard, patchy grass, and no patio furniture. No toys. No sign of a dog or cat. I circled back toward the side of the garage, where a small window gave me a view inside.

No vehicle. Just stacks of cardboard boxes piled high, leaving little room to park a car. It confirmed my suspicion that Slade had gone somewhere that night, met our perp, and somehow ended up in that chimney.

The crime scene unit van pulled up in the driveway, and I headed over to greet the team to start the search of the home.

Two hours later, three crime scene techs and I finished searching Garrett Slade's home. We didn't find anything out of the ordinary or anything to point to who may have wanted to hurt Slade, but we had found a laptop. The team would try to get in and see if there was anything useful on it.

After the team left, I headed next door and knocked. A young woman, maybe in her twenties, answered.

"Hi, can I help you?"

I showed her my badge. "My name is Detective Maddox. I'm investigating a crime involving your next-door neighbor. Did you know him?"

Her eyes widened slightly. "Did something happen to him?"

"I'm afraid so. Do you know if he has any family or friends in the area?"

She shook her head. "No. I didn't know him very well. He mostly kept to himself. Always friendly though. He'd wave when I saw him in the yard."

"How long have you lived here?"

"About five years."

I nodded. "Anything unusual happen over the last week or two? Any strange cars or people loitering who didn't look like they fit in the area?"

She shook her head again.

"Do you have any surveillance cameras on your house?"

"No. But I know a few of the neighbors do."

"All right, I'll check with them." I thanked her for her time, jotted her information in my notebook, and moved on to the next house. Same story, Mr. Slade was friendly enough, but the neighbors had no useful information that pointed to a motive. I crossed the street to the house directly opposite Slade's.

A man, probably in his seventies, answered. "Hello?"

"Hi, my name is Detective Maddox. How are you, sir?"

He adjusted his glasses. "I'm okay. What can I help you with, Detective?"

"I'm investigating a crime relating to your neighbor across the street, Garrett Slade. Did you know him?"

"Well, not too well. We talked sometimes when we were both out working in the yard."

"How long have you lived here?"

He stepped forward and looked over at Slade's home. "Oh, about thirty years."

"Then you knew Mr. Slade when he had foster children living with him?"

"Oh yeah. Back when his wife was still with us. A lot of kids in and out. Not lately. I think they gave that up a few years before she died."

"Did you know Mrs. Slade?"

"A little. She didn't get out much either, but when I stopped seeing her, I did go over and ask if everything was okay. Being neighborly and all. That's when I learned she passed. He seemed pretty sad."

"Do you remember if he had any visitors recently?"

"Not that I noticed. Far as I can tell, he has kept to himself since his wife died."

"Do you know if he leaves the house much? I understand he's retired."

"Yeah, he goes out. Doesn't tell me where, but he usually goes somewhere every day. Surprises me, too, given he's retired."

"Do you remember, back when he had the kids, if there were any fights or anything strange going on?"

"Not that I recall. I mean, they're kids, so sometimes they were kinda loud if I remember correctly. But no fights that stick out in my mind. I think they only had a few kids at a time."

"Anything else you could tell me? Anything unusual happen recently?"

He shook his head. "No."

"Do you have a Ring camera or any other surveillance on your home?"

"I do. Would you like to take a look?"

"Yes, that would be very helpful. Thank you."

"Come on in and I'll get that all squared away for you."

I stepped inside and the faint scent of coffee lingered in the air, mingled with the sweet, stale aroma of old pipe tobacco. The carpet was worn but clean, its beige color faded in high-traffic spots. Family photos crowded the walls, sepia-toned wedding portraits, school pictures in mismatched frames, and a few candid snapshots of children playing in a backyard.

"What's your name?" I asked as we passed a side table stacked with mail and a porcelain lamp topped by a yellowing shade.

"My name is Terry Blatchard, but you can call me Butch."

"Thanks, Butch. You live here alone?"

His voice lowered. "I do now. My wife passed last year."

"I'm so sorry for your loss."

"Thankfully my kids visit a lot. You got any kids?"

"No." *Not yet—likely not ever.*

He led me into a small study. Shelves filled with well-worn books and rows of VHS tapes. A desk sat against the far wall, a desktop computer on its surface. He lowered himself into the chair and began tapping at the keyboard.

My cell phone vibrated in my pocket. "This is Maddox."

A voice on the other end was urgent. "We've got another body." *Well, merry freakin' Christmas.*

7

DETECTIVE KATE MADDOX

The crime scene was inside the bottom level apartment of an old Victorian home in Oakland. Outside the entrance, a pale, wide-eyed older man stood beside Officer Ogden. The older man's hands trembled as he muttered, "Never smelled anything like it." He was likely the apartment manager who had called it in.

"I understand, sir," Ogden told him. "It's very unpleasant. You don't need to be here if you have somewhere else to be. We're taking the scene."

The man gave a jerky nod and backed away, still rattled, but clearly relieved to be out of there. Once he left, I walked up to Ogden and he opened the door. The stench hit me, thick, clinging, and unmistakable. Death.

Ogden motioned for me to go inside, "We've got another interesting one for you."

I raised an eyebrow.

"Another Christmas present," he said grimly. "Brace yourself. Crime scene techs are already in there and it's a tight space."

With a nod, I pulled my scarf a little higher over my nose and entered into a small living room with a tattered sofa, coffee table, television from the late nineties, and a small dining table. Next to it was a kitchenette. A door ajar looked like it was a bedroom. Another door was kept open, and I could see a crime scene tech kneeling next to the tub with a camera. Outside stood Jeff, the head of the CSU team.

"Hey, Jeff," I said quietly. "What've we got in there?"

He exhaled slowly. "Believe it or not, it's more gruesome than the last. Much more gruesome. Brace yourself."

"Is the M.E. here yet?"

He shook his head. "She's on her way."

"Thanks."

I slipped booties over my shoes, pulled gloves onto my hands, and stepped into the bathroom.

An elderly woman lay in a shallow bath of murky water, dark red and clouded. Her gray hair spread like a fan around her head. Around the tub, someone had strung multicolored Christmas lights. They blinked on and off, throwing red and green glimmers across the water's surface. On the edge of the tub sat a tiny, one-foot Christmas tree, its miniature ornaments catching the light with a sparkle that felt all wrong in this place.

I moved in closer. There were what looked like restraint marks around her wrists. Her face was slashed with so many cuts and abrasions I had to force myself to catalog them, one at a time. Dark bruises spread across her shoulders and chest.

If she'd been awake, she would've been in unimaginable agony. If she'd been drugged, it might have been enough to spare her. The mix of brutality and holiday décor was deeply disturbing.

She lived in an apartment, beneath other tenants. If she'd screamed, they might have heard her. But when the call came in, it wasn't about screams. It was about the smell, the smell that led the landlord to unlock the door and find her like this.

I stepped out of the bathroom. I'd seen enough. The only

apparent exit and entrance was the front door. I walked back over to Ogden who stood outside. I glanced up and around the building. "I don't see any surveillance cameras. Did you ask the apartment manager if there were any?"

"There aren't."

Mulling over the scene, I thought aloud, "Someone could've snuck in when she wasn't home. She came home, he drugged and killed her, and walked right out. Or she let him in. Maybe she knew her killer."

He nodded. "The Christmas lights. The tree. What do you think?"

"Another Christmas-themed murder. Did you find any notes? Or Christmas cards?"

"I didn't see anything when I first came in," Ogden said, "but you can ask the techs."

I waved Jeff over. "Did you find any notes, cards, or messages?"

"Nope," he said. "Just the body, the Christmas lights, and the tree. Doesn't look like there was any forced entry on the door either. She either let her killer in... or she was killed somewhere else and placed in the tub."

Thinking back to the bathroom, the tiles were relatively clean. "There would've been a lot of blood," I said slowly. "Unless they killed her in the tub and then filled it with water."

Jeff gave a small nod.

"Do we know who the victim is?" I asked Ogden.

He nodded. "Sixty-two-year-old Margaret Ellison. According to the landlord, she's retired from Oakland Child Protective Services."

That caught my attention. The last victim had been a foster parent. Now we had a retired CPS worker. That wasn't a coincidence. And neither were the Christmas decorations.

My heartbeat kicked up a notch. This was something, maybe

a tenuous connection with the chimney murder, but a connection nonetheless. There would be a lot of names to go through. A CPS worker could have hundreds of children they were responsible for overseeing in foster care. We needed a list of Ms. Ellison's kids to match them up with the Slades'. It might be exactly what we needed to break the case, or at least narrow down the potential suspects. Was someone, a former foster kid, seeking revenge? If that were true, most kids had more than one foster home. And then a thought hit me like a grenade. *Our killer might not be finished.*

8

MARTINA

The sun was shining despite the chilly air. Charlie and I strolled side by side as we walked Barney. He had to stop at every single bush, light post, or object to sniff and investigate. I liked to think that if Barney were human, he'd be a private investigator too.

Was this a sign I might be losing my mind, thinking about if Barney were an actual person? Maybe I needed to go back to work. Too much time off, and I'd start turning into a crazy dog lady.

Charlie broke my thoughts. "Excited for Zoey to come home?"

"I am. Just a few more days before she flies in. I can't wait."

"We're going to have a full house this year."

"It's exciting, isn't it?"

"It is. What should we do today?"

"We can go on a hike after we settle Barney in, then have lunch."

"Sounds nice. It's perfect hiking weather."

"It is." Could this be my life all the time? At some point, I would have to retire, right? Could I just spend my days hiking, walking the dog, and reading the paper? Did I need a hobby? I certainly didn't have one other than investigating crimes or missing persons. What kind of hobby could I have? I could volunteer. It had been a while since I'd helped at the recovery center, the place where I'd met Charlie all those years ago. I smiled to myself at the thought. It wasn't love at first sight, but it was pretty close.

"You know," Charlie said, "we could always feed Barney, and then I could put together a picnic lunch. We could hike up Pleasanton Ridge or go to Sunol and have a picnic."

"That sounds lovely."

"Plus, we still have cookies left over from your mom's. That'll give us the sugar we need to hike back."

"It's a date," I said with a grin.

Barney bounded forward and sniffed our mailbox.

It was kind of nice having no plans. With Charlie's career as an author, he had a lot of flexibility in his schedule. If I had time off, he could take time off. It worked out well.

"I'll grab the mail," Charlie said. "Do you want to bring Barney in?"

With a nod, I said, "Come on, Barney."

Barney bounded up to the front door. He was probably hungry; it was lunchtime. Charlie had been making him special food lately. Apparently, he'd read an article about how some dog food companies don't use the finest ingredients, so he decided to start making homemade meals for him. I don't think that dog could be any more spoiled.

We entered through the door, and Barney ran straight to his water dish. Charlie followed shortly behind.

I looked at his hands, which held the stack of mail from the mailbox. I thought I saw a red envelope peeking out from among the white ones. "Anything for me?"

He sorted through the mail. "Another red envelope with your name on it. No return address."

I didn't like that, not one bit. Who was sending me these cards? What would I find when I opened this one? Should I wait to open it and have it fingerprinted? Or was I just being paranoid? Perhaps it was too many years as a private investigator making me think everything could be evidence.

Inside the kitchen, I paused, leaning against the counter. I opened the envelope and pulled out the Christmas card. This one had Christmas lights hung from a red and white two-story house and a decorated tree next to the door. It was pretty, actually. I opened it.

The pre-printed message read:

Wishing you the merriest of holiday seasons.

Underneath, in blocky handwritten letters:

SHE TOOK SO MUCH FROM ME AND MANY OTHERS. YOU HAVE TO LET THEM SEE. SHOW THEM.

In the bottom right-hand corner—again—that small, hand-drawn snowflake.

A powerful feeling came over me. My pulse quickened and I went straight to my phone and searched for any recent homicides. I stopped scrolling when I saw the headline: "*A Second Unsolved Christmas Killing Leaves Oakland Neighbors Shaken.*" After a quiet gasp, I began to read.

~

A SECOND UNSOLVED CHRISTMAS KILLING LEAVES OAKLAND NEIGHBORS SHAKEN

By Natalie Sloane – The Bay Insider

OAKLAND, Calif. — On December 14, sixty-two-year-old Margaret "Maggie" Ellison was found dead in her East Oakland apartment home. The discovery came after neighbors called the property manager to complain about a foul odor seeping into the hallway. When he unlocked the door, the smell grew overwhelming, and in the dim light, he saw the bathtub surrounded by Christmas lights.

Maggie's body was submerged in frigid water. Sources tell The Bay Insider she had suffered extensive blunt-force injuries, burns, and restraint marks. The coroner has not released a cause of death.

It's impossible to ignore the disturbing similarities to the 2010 Kristy Bamu case in London, in which a fifteen-year-old boy was tortured and drowned by relatives, on Christmas day, who claimed they were "purging evil" from him. Was Maggie targeted because of a similar belief? Or was her death staged to look like a ritual? At this point, police will not comment on motive. No arrests have been made.

Maggie was a retired employee of Oakland's Child Protective Services. For decades, she worked with some of the city's most vulnerable children, advocating for their safety in the often-overwhelmed foster care system. This is the second violent Christmas-themed, unsolved death in the Bay Area in the weeks leading up to Christmas. Whether the similarities between the cases are coincidence or a connection remains unclear, but the pattern is growing harder to ignore.

The holidays are supposed to be a time of peace, yet these killings are proof that December can be just as dangerous as any other month, sometimes more so, when stress and old grudges boil over. If you hear something, say something. You might save a life. And if the person responsible is reading this, remember, secrets have a way of surfacing. The city is watching. I'm watching.

∼

To say I was shook was an understatement. What did this mean? Were the eerie Christmas cards connected to the murders? After I reread the article, another article popped up.

∽

VICTIM IN OAKLAND 'SANTA CHIMNEY' CASE IDENTIFIED

By Natalie Sloane – The Bay Insider

OAKLAND, Calif. — Authorities have identified the victim in last week's grisly "Santa in the chimney" homicide as 67-year-old Garrett Slade, a former foster parent and longtime employee at Adams Point Grocery.

Slade's body was discovered Thursday morning lodged in the chimney of a vacant property in the Adams Point area. Dressed in a full Santa suit, his death has drawn both media and community attention for its eerie resemblance to urban legends and real-life holiday tragedies.

The Oakland Police Department has declined to elaborate on the circumstances of his death or whether any suspects have been identified. "Right now, our priority is piecing together Mr. Slade's final hours and determining who may have wanted to harm him," a representative of the Oakland Police Department said. "This was a deliberate act. Someone put him there."

The police are asking the public to come forward if they knew Mr. Slade or knew of his whereabouts on the night of December 11. Anyone with information is urged to contact the Oakland Police Department's homicide tip line.

∽

My pulse quickened and I could feel the adrenaline shooting through my veins as I reread the first article. One victim had been a foster parent. The second victim had worked for Child Protective Services. That had to be more than a coincidence.

Without thinking another thought, I picked up the phone and called the one person I knew would give me sound advice. Maybe I was reading too much into this. Maybe I'd had too much time off and was looking for something, anything, to solve.

He answered after the second ring. "Hey, Martina."

"Hi, Hirsch. I have a bad feeling about something. Do you mind if I run it by you?"

"Of course. What's up?"

I explained that I'd gotten the first red envelope the same day I read about the first murder, the chimney murder in Oakland, and that earlier, I'd received a second envelope after the news broke about the woman found dead in her bathtub. "What do you think?"

"I think we should reach out to the Oakland police department and let them know you're getting these notes. It could be absolutely nothing, or it could be connected. It's a little strange, I have to admit, especially based on the timing. You know I don't believe in coincidences, Martina."

"I don't either. Do you have any contacts at Oakland PD? I don't think I've ever worked with anyone over there. Sheriff's Department in Alameda County, sure, but not OPD."

"I know a few people. I can find out who the detective on the case is, could be the same person working both murders. Let me make a few calls and I'll call you right back."

"Okay."

The call ended, and I felt a hand on my lower back. "Everything okay?" Charlie asked.

"I'm not so sure." I explained to him everything I'd just told Hirsch, and what Hirsch was doing.

Charlie let out a breath. "You can take the private investigator out of the office, but you can't take the crimes away from the private investigator, huh?"

"It could be nothing, but I think the OPD detective should know about this just in case there is a connection."

"I agree. But..."

"But what?"

"I mean, you're just going to hand it off to them, right?"

"I don't know. I don't really know much about it yet. It could be nothing, like I said. Could be somebody saw the articles and is just trying to mess with me."

"Is that what you think is happening? What's your gut saying, Martina?"

I closed my eyes and shook my head. "I've got a feeling, Charlie. I don't think it's a coincidence. And if these murders are connected, I don't think they're going to stop."

"What are you going to do about it?"

He gave me a look, the one that said, "You're going to work this case even if it's not yours, aren't you?" I knew the look. How could I turn my back if they needed me? Of course I would have to help. Before I could answer, my phone rang again. "Hey, Hirsch."

"Okay, so I talked to an old OPD friend of mine. Said the detective on the case is Kate Maddox, she's working both of them."

"I should go see her in person."

"You could just call her and tell her what you found."

"But what if the cards are evidence? She'll want them, right?"

"True," he said, like he didn't quite believe that was my only reason.

"I'm serious. If you were the detective on the case, wouldn't you want any pertinent evidence?"

"I would. Do you want me to go down there with you?"

"No. I'm sure it will be a quick trip."

"Okay, well, I told her to expect you and I'll send you her details. You can give her a call before you arrive."

He knows me too well. "Thanks, Hirsch."

"Keep me posted. I don't like the idea of some creep leaving you cards in your mailbox, because that means they know where you live."

That was true. How did they find out where I lived? I'd worked hard to keep all my personal details private. "All right, Hirsch, I'll let you know how it goes."

"Be safe, Martina."

After I ended the call, Charlie gave me a look. "Is our hike canceled?"

I gave him a look back, but no answer.

"How about I fix some sandwiches? You can head out and go talk to that detective, and we can go on a hike tomorrow. Or if you're back early enough, we can go later."

"You're the best, Charlie."

"Yes. Yes, I am."

I wrapped my arms around him and kissed him. The knots in my stomach told me I might be walking into something dangerous, but also something important. As I grabbed my coat and the two red envelopes, the snowflake symbols burned in my mind. If these murders were connected, the killer wasn't just sending a message to the police. They were sending it to me. But why?

9

HIM

I read the headline again. "Victim in Oakland 'Santa Chimney' Case Identified." Garrett Slade. I let the name roll in my mind. Natalie had written it plainly, without knowing the weight it carried. She had listed his jobs, his years at Adams Point Grocery, the foster children he had taken in. She hadn't said what kind of man he was. Not yet. My eyes lingered on her phrasing, someone put him there. A smile tugged at the corner of my mouth. Yes, someone had. And soon the world would know his name for all the lies he'd hidden behind.

Natalie was helping me strip away the mask, piece by piece. *She's getting closer.* But she was still missing the most important part, the why. But I wouldn't give her that, not yet.

The second article made me sit forward. Maggie Ellison... bathtub... Christmas lights. Natalie had described the scene almost perfectly. It wasn't likely that she'd been there, but her words painted the picture exactly the way I wanted the public to see it. She'd even drawn the parallel to the Kristy Bamu case. *Clever girl.* Then I reached the last lines. "If the person responsible is reading this, remember, secrets have a way of surfacing. The city is watching. *I'm watching.*"

With a grimace, I said to myself, "Oh, I know you're watching, Natalie. Perhaps I should be watching you."

I ran a finger under her byline again. She thought her warning was a threat, but to me, it was an invitation. She was writing directly to me, acknowledging me, and speaking into the dark where she knew I would be listening. That was how connections were made. That was how trust was built. I carefully cut out both articles with slow precision and tacked them up on the cork board with the rest of my collection.

They'll know the truth soon enough. And I have a feeling my new friend, Natalie, would be the one to tell them. I was sure she would, so our time together could wait. I needed to check on my other helper. Everything inside me knew she would discover the truth and seek justice for the victims. Death wasn't enough for them. And the crimes wouldn't end with them, that was why I needed Martina. *Has she begun to understand her role?*

10

MARTINA

I stepped through the doors of the Oakland Police Department and walked up to the receptionist. "Hi, my name is Martina Monroe and I'm here to see Detective Maddox."

The young man seated behind the desk said, "Is she expecting you?"

"Yes, I have an appointment."

"Just a moment, please. Here, fill this out, and I'll need your ID as well."

I nodded, took the clipboard, and began filling out the form. As I slid my driver's license from my wallet, I couldn't help wondering what Detective Maddox was like. Was she competent? Good at her job? I knew nothing about her, and the thought left me curious, and maybe a little uneasy.

The man hung up the phone and glanced my way. "Detective Maddox will be right out. You can have a seat."

"Thanks."

I couldn't. Sitting felt impossible. My adrenaline was soaring, my body preparing for whatever came next. I paced, letting my gaze roam the lobby. In the far corner stood a Giving Tree, decorated with paper tags that listed a child's Christmas wish, waiting for someone to take it, buy the gift, and return it for delivery, a secret Santa of sorts. It was a lovely thought. Maybe we should do something similar at Drakos Monroe. Too late for this season, but something to plan for next year. I leaned closer, scanning the requests. Most of them were from children and teens, many from foster homes. And just like that, my thoughts were back on the two articles. Two victims: a foster parent, and a CPS worker.

From over my shoulder, a voice called, "Martina Monroe?"

I turned to see a woman approaching.

"I'm Detective Maddox," she said, extending her hand.

We shook.

She was a little younger than me, mid-to-late thirties. Average height. Pretty, but in an unconventional way. Her dark eyes seemed a little haunted, as though she carried the weight of every case she'd worked. Her life likely hadn't been easy. Something had driven her to become a homicide detective. It wasn't usually a carefree childhood. And honestly, I was curious to know more about her.

"Why don't you come back with me? We've got a conference room where we can talk."

As I followed her through the bullpen, the air buzzed with activity. Officers hunched over desks tapped out reports, while others leaned in close during tense conversations. A few people sat in chairs against the wall, their postures telling me they were either witnesses, or perpetrators.

Inside the conference room, she closed the door behind us. "Come on in. Please, have a seat."

I settled into the chair across from her as she opened a notebook. "I was told by a colleague that you have some messages that may be related to the recent murders. The chimney murder and..."

"The Christmas killing in the bathtub," I finished for her.

She nodded. "So, what do you have? What messages have you received?"

I reached into my bag and pulled out a large Ziploc containing both Christmas cards. I took them out and set them on the table. "Honestly, I didn't think they were evidence when I first got them," I admitted. "So, I didn't wear gloves or anything. My prints will be all over them. My husband's too."

"Yeah, it's probably a bit late now," she said. "Were they sealed?"

"No."

I knew what she was thinking, DNA from the sender's saliva on the envelope. But there'd be no luck there. She opened the first card and read silently. Her expression shifted, surprise, maybe even recognition.

"What is it?" I asked.

"Just... a bit chilling," she said, her tone guarded. She was holding something back. She didn't trust me. She picked up the second card, read it, then placed both hands flat on the table and looked me directly in the eyes. "Any idea who sent these to you?"

"I have no idea. But from my thirty years in private investigations and working on cold cases with the CoCo County Sheriff's Department, I'd guess it's somebody who wants my help. They want me to find something and expose it. And the timing, both cards arriving right after the Christmas-themed murders, makes me think they're connected."

She eyed me. "I've heard of your firm, Drakos Monroe Security & Investigations."

"And I used to contract with CoCo County to solve cold cases."

She nodded. "There's not much I can tell you, it's an active investigation, but what I can say is, I have reason to believe the two crimes might be connected and your messages might be related."

"How so?"

"I'm sorry, Martina. I can't divulge that."

I sat back, my mind racing. I couldn't just sit there quietly. If this killer was reaching out to me, how could I hand it all over to the police and walk away? I knew she didn't know me, and I didn't know her, but maybe that needed to change. "Look," I said, "I read the articles in The Bay Insider. The first victim was a foster parent. The second, a retired member of Child Protective Services. Now someone wants me to uncover something, to show the truth. They're connected."

"We have our suspicions. Nothing concrete."

"I'm telling you, it's the same killer. And I don't think they're going to stop. I probably shouldn't even be doing this. I'm supposed to be on vacation. But I can help. I'm guessing you're looking into foster kids that the two victims had contact with. There's probably a lot of names to go through. Am I right so far?"

She let out a breath and averted her gaze.

"Look, I'm not someone who sits on the sidelines. A number of law enforcement officers can vouch for me. I've worked for the Sheriff's Department. This killer is in my world. You saw the envelopes, there is no return address and no stamp. They were put directly in my mailbox, at my house. You can accept my help, and we can work together, or I'll investigate on my own because I don't want this guy at my house or near my family."

Detective Maddox crossed her arms, leaned back in her chair, and studied me. "This is an active investigation."

"And my guess is, you need help," I countered. "Oakland has the highest homicide rate in the state of California. I'm sure you're up to your eyeballs in crime. I'm offering help pro bono. I'll sign a contract, whatever you need. But I'm not backing away from this. Detective Maddox, I don't back down from threats against my family."

She remained silent.

"I'll admit, I don't know how I'm connected to this. I don't know why this person has reached out to me. I haven't figured it out yet, but I will."

She studied me. "What was the arrangement when you worked for CoCo County?"

"When they started a new cold case division, I contracted with them to work full-time on cold cases. I had a contract, I was paid, and I was essentially a representative of the Sheriff's Department. I followed their rules. At my firm, I don't have as many rules, but if you accept my help and you want to work together, I'll follow yours." *When I can.*

"I have to run this by my boss."

"I'm offering my help," I said, leaning in slightly. "And I could probably chip in some of my researchers, too. I'm a partner at my firm. I've got top-notch people, the best there is at finding people, digging into backgrounds, figuring out where they are, what they do, and who they know. And based on what my stepdaughter, Selena, told me on the way over, both of these cases have gone viral on TikTok, Instagram, all the social media channels. You're getting a lot of pressure to solve them. Bringing me in could make for some good headlines."

She continued to eye me skeptically.

"I don't know if you've checked into me, but I have quite the record for solving tough cases." I watched her eyes. She still wasn't sold. Honestly, I didn't think it would be such a tough sell. My track record should have her begging for my help. But maybe she had trust issues. I could understand that. "I'll sign whatever you want."

She looked me over once more. "I've gotta talk to my boss, but... let's just say we could use your help. And yeah, it's not helping with social media. All kinds of conspiracy theories about these Christmas killings. I know the reporter covering them, she's reliable, doesn't leak what we don't want leaked."

"Natalie Sloane?"

"Yes. We're friends. I usually give her the first take on my cases. She respects boundaries. Doesn't try to sneak into crime scenes. That kind of thing."

I gave a small nod.

"So I guess what I'm saying is, on a trial basis, I'll accept your help, if my boss is on board. If he agrees, you'll have to follow the rules, because whoever is doing this needs to be behind bars. We can't let him slip on a technicality."

"Any physical evidence collected? Any idea who this guy is?"

She shut her eyes briefly and shook her head.

"I didn't think so. I have a feeling this guy's been planning this, whatever *this* is, for a long time. And my biggest fear is, he's just getting started."

Detective Maddox met my eyes. "Mine too. Give me a minute, I'll be right back."

Detective Maddox left the conference room. Despite her reluctance, I had a good feeling about her. She wanted to do right by the victims, and so did I. We needed to stop this guy, and I had a feeling she needed my help to do it. Hopefully, her boss could see that.

A few minutes later, she returned with a small smile. "My boss is okay with you helping, but he wants it to be official."

"I can do official."

With a grin we shook on it.

Sure, there would be paperwork and conversations that would follow, but I believed that together we would solve this case and stop the madman. I just hoped we could do it before he claimed his next victim.

11

DETECTIVE KATE MADDOX

After Martina stepped out of the room to make a phone call, I leaned back in my chair and tried to figure out how we could best work together. I'd never partnered with a consultant, or a non-law enforcement professional, on a case before. Over drinks, it wasn't uncommon for Natalie and I to toss around a few hypothetical scenarios about a case. Natalie was a friend, someone I trusted. I didn't know Martina, and I wasn't sure how I would like working with her. Or anyone, if I were being honest.

When I told my boss, Tatum, about her offer to help us, he'd practically wet his pants. Apparently, he'd heard of her firm and had been buddies with her best pal and investigative partner, retired Sergeant Hirsch. If she was as good as everyone claimed, I'll be impressed. But for now, I'd proceed with cautious optimism.

The door opened and Martina stepped back in, phone in hand, eyes sharp and assessing. "So, should we get started?"

Right to the chase. I liked it. "Sure."

"Do you have a situation room? A murder board? How do you usually run your investigations?"

She didn't waste time on pleasantries, just dove straight in. This working relationship might just work after all. "We don't currently. It's just been me working the case. It's a busy time of year," I said, shifting in my seat.

"Okay. Well, I typically have a whole team, but if it's just you and me to start, I can always bring in my people if we need extra help. Like I said, we need to get this guy. He knows where *I* live. My family's coming for the holidays and I can't be getting notes from a serial killer. It takes some of the jolly out of our merry Christmas. You know what I mean?"

Her words tumbled out quickly, but her eyes stayed locked on mine, searching for any hint of doubt. "I do. I could probably get a conference room dedicated to us, and we could start from there. How does this one work?" I asked, glancing around the small conference room.

She looked around and I followed her gaze. I didn't know what she was used to at her fancy firm, but this was probably all we could spare. It wasn't the greatest space considering it smelled faintly of stale coffee and sweat. The conference room doubled as our interview space for suspects and witnesses. We didn't have a lot of extra rooms to throw around. Still, she'd said the words I'd been thinking too. Serial killer. We didn't have one, yet, but I feared we might.

We only knew of two deaths that I was fairly certain were connected, but not one hundred percent. The fact Martina had gotten two letters, both with the same snowflake in the bottom corner like the one left at the first scene, made me think it had to be connected. Between that and a hunch our killer wasn't finished, I grew wary more festively wrapped bodies would turn up.

Martina leaned forward, forearms braced on the table. "Can I see what you have so far on the case?"

"Of course. Give me a sec." I stood up and hurried back to

my desk. My hands were steady, but my stomach felt tight as I grabbed the files and the photos from both crime scenes. Anyone who looked at those images and didn't flinch either had ice in their veins or had seen far too much. Despite all I'd seen in my career, I was still somewhere in between.

Back in the conference room, I spread the files across the table. Martina didn't recoil. Instead, she leaned over the chimney murder photos, her expression unreadable. "Is the autopsy on the first victim done yet?"

"Yeah. He died of asphyxia due to his head being wrapped in tape after a blunt-force trauma to the skull," I said, my voice sounding flatter than I intended. "Then he was dressed in the Santa suit and shoved up the chimney."

Martina's mouth pressed into a thin line. She didn't flinch and didn't blink. She just kept her eyes locked on the crime scene photos as if willing them to give up more than they were. "Any idea where Mr. Slade was the day before he died?"

"We canvassed his neighborhood. People said he kept to himself. I had my reporter friend do a follow-up article to see if anybody else knew where he might have been the night he was killed and if they did, to come forward. We couldn't find any family or next of kin. His wife died about five years ago. We don't know where he was the night before he died, but we've got a BOLO on his vehicle. It still hasn't been located."

She cocked her head. "Could be a chance meeting... but the fact that the other murder is a CPS worker makes me think it wasn't."

"I don't think it was a chance meeting either."

"No fingerprints at the scene? Fibers? Anything connecting to a suspect?"

I shook my head.

Her eyes narrowed. "And how about this one?" She tapped a

photo of the second victim's crime scene with a fingernail. "This is horrific. Was she drugged too?"

"Thankfully, yes."

She released a slow breath. "That's something. Any idea how old the wounds are?"

"At first, we thought maybe she'd been tortured over a long period of time, but the medical examiner thinks they were all done in a relatively short window. We have a theory he was trying to mimic a previous crime that occurred in 2010." I glanced at her, half-expecting a flicker of surprise. *Nothing.* "He's re-creating crimes committed at Christmas time. The question is why."

She nodded, "Any physical evidence from the second crime scene?"

"No hits yet."

"No fingerprints, no hairs? No footprints?"

"Nope. It's like he's a ghost."

She finally looked up at me. "No physical evidence at the scene, that's unusual."

"There is evidence he cleaned up afterward," I said. "The only gruesome details are the bodies themselves and how they're placed."

"And they were placed," she echoed, almost under her breath. "What was the female victim's cause of death?"

"Likely manual strangulation, but she died of asphyxiation."

"Were the wounds inflicted postmortem?"

"No."

"That makes sense, there's bleeding," she said as she leaned closer to the photo. She seemed to catalogue every angle, and every mark, as though building the killer in her head piece by piece.

"Have you ever been to an autopsy?" I asked.

She nodded faintly. "They're not my favorite activity."

I sat back, studying her. Maybe Martina Monroe really was all she was cracked up to be.

"Both technically died of asphyxiation," I continued. "One from the tape, one from manual strangulation. It's interesting. It's almost as if he didn't want his victims to suffer."

"Maybe it's not about sparing them," Martina said. "Maybe it's about keeping them quiet. Doing what he wants without interference. Being able to place them somewhere specific. Maybe he doesn't have a place to keep them, so he kills them in their homes. Or, in the case of the chimney murder, in a vacant house. It's possible he switched from blunt force to strangulation so there would be less to clean up."

"It's possible."

"Motive?"

"Our first victim hadn't had a foster child in at least ten years. If it's one of his foster kids seeking revenge, that's a long time to hold a grudge and do nothing. Something had to have triggered him."

"But what?" she asked, still studying the photo.

"That's a good question."

"Have you searched for similar crimes in the area?"

"We've definitely looked for crimes on or around Christmas over the last five years, nothing local."

"Something triggered this killer," she repeated.

"Something around the holidays," I said.

"Maybe last year, and he's spent this year planning it out."

"It's a good theory."

"Have you started doing backgrounds on all the foster children the first victim had in his home and then cross checked the retired CPS victim's case files?"

She seemed to know how to run an investigation. That was good to know. "We've pulled names and are waiting on the former CPS worker case files."

"It's most likely our killer grew up in the foster system. From what I understand, a lot of foster homes aren't exactly a safe haven."

I smirked. "That," I said, "I am, unfortunately, well aware."

She cocked her head, her gaze softening. "You grew up in the system?"

"Since I was seven."

Her brows drew together. "I'm so sorry."

"It was a long time ago." I said it like it didn't matter, but the truth was, I could still smell the musty carpet of that first foster home, still hear the hollow creak of the hallway outside my bedroom as my foster father approached.

She studied me for a beat. "Then you understand—the foster angle is probably our best bet."

"I do. But there's a lot to dig through."

"Well, like I mentioned, I'm willing to lend out some of my team members. We can split up the list, do background checks, start knocking on doors, and checking alibis. Chances are, some of them are no longer alive and maybe some are incarcerated. It could narrow it down for us."

I gave a grim nod. "Unfortunately, a lot of foster kids don't have a high success rate. Nationally, only about half graduate high school. Maybe three or four percent ever get a four-year college degree. Around one in four end up incarcerated within just a couple years of aging out, and the numbers for overdose or early death aren't much better."

Martina's eyes softened. "You were an exception."

I shrugged. "They told me I was one of the lucky ones," I said. "That I'd survived the system and somehow turned out okay. But that wasn't the case for a lot of the kids I knew. It's hard to overcome that kind of trauma, especially when the very place that's supposed to protect you can hurt you in ways you don't come back from."

Why was I telling her this? She had a way about her that made you believe she cared about you. Is this how she gets information from witnesses and suspects?

"Then you know better than anyone," she said, leaning forward, "that one of those names could lead us straight to our killer."

"Exactly. Somebody's been carrying this grudge for a long time, and something triggered them to act now."

"Check the list and find the trigger. Between those two, we'll find our killer," she said.

"I agree."

She gave me a small, knowing smile. Maybe working with a partner wouldn't be so bad after all. And if it meant we caught the killer before he could hurt anyone else, I'd call it a Christmas miracle.

12

HIM

The street outside her house glowed faintly, the cold air turning the Christmas lights into soft halos. She'd strung them along the roofline in perfect lines, warm white, no blinking, the kind that made the place look safe and inviting.

I'd been watching for hours, hidden inside my car parked across the street. The lights from inside told me her husband was home. I'd seen him pass by the window earlier. But not her.

She'd left before I'd arrived. I'd assumed she'd be home shortly, considering when I called her office they'd informed me she'd been on vacation and would be throughout the holiday season. Had she gone into the office to investigate the crimes? Had she understood my messages?

I needed her to understand and expose them. I couldn't trust the police to do it. Perhaps between the reporter Natalie Sloane and her, they could solve the case. Perhaps I needed to bring them together. Hmm. *A challenge.*

Natalie Sloane had understood my message. Every word she typed had been like a breadcrumb leading her toward something bigger. Could she be my messenger? Two were better than one. I'd need to get them together. But how?

Headlights swept the street, and I lowered myself into the vehicle, and peeked above the seat. A car turned into her driveway and parked. It was her.

She climbed out slowly, her breath puffing in the cold. The keys in her hand caught the glow of the porch lights. Where had she been? The door closed behind her and she was out of sight.

The Christmas lights of the Monroe home and those of her neighbors were bright against the night, while I stayed in the dark. Waiting.

13

MARTINA

Back inside the conference room at the Oakland Police Department, I studied the list Detective Maddox had given me. The paper was curled at the edges and names were highlighted in three different colors. There were seventy-five foster children who had been in Garrett Slade and his wife Virginia's home. By the time I'd arrived that morning, Detective Maddox had already split them into deceased, incarcerated, and alive. She must've worked all night. I glanced at my watch, it was 8 AM. "Detective Maddox, did you go home last night?" I asked, eyeing her wrinkled blouse and the blazer draped over the back of her chair.

"You can call me Kate."

"Okay, Kate. Did you go home last night?"

"No, but I took a break, had dinner and drinks with a friend, then came back."

"That's an excellent way to burn out."

She shot me a look over the rim of her coffee cup, the kind that said, "Don't start with me."

"And not working," she said, "is a good way to let a killer catch another victim."

"True," I said, holding up my hands in surrender. "But your physical health matters. Working all night takes a toll."

Kate's lips pressed into a thin line, the muscles in her jaw twitching. She didn't like being mothered. I could practically feel the annoyance coming off her.

"Well, let's hope we catch him soon," she said, eyes back on the papers.

I nodded and looked over the list. "Okay, so out of these, twenty are deceased, twenty-two are incarcerated. That leaves thirty-three that could be our suspect. Did you pull backgrounds on all thirty-three?"

"I've completed ten." She pushed another stack toward me. "Of the ten, nine have last known addresses. The other may be unhoused or deceased but not identified. The other twenty-three I'm still working on. Doing this alone takes time."

"If you'd told me you were working, I could've helped."

"You have a family, right?"

I nodded.

"I don't," she said quickly. "It's fine."

"You don't have anyone? You said you met a friend for dinner."

"Yeah. The reporter I told you about."

"No cat? No dog? Not even a goldfish?"

"Nope. My job is my family."

"A job isn't a family," I said, softer this time, my thoughts flicking to Selena. She had family and friends, but was a workaholic. Kate kind of reminded me of her.

Kate's eyes lifted briefly, before she shut the door on the topic. "Let's just focus on the case."

I worried about Kate. She had to be tough to survive on her own all these years, but at this pace, she'd burn out, make a mistake, or get herself killed. Or drink herself to death like too many cops, and a few PIs, who couldn't draw a line between the job and their life. I would know.

But I wouldn't push. I understood the need to solve a case. And being a female homicide detective in a male-dominated department probably meant she had to work twice as hard to prove herself, maybe that's why she worked alone.

"Okay," I said, "you have nine for us to contact. Should we call them? How do you think we're most likely to get ahold of them?"

"I think we need to find them and talk in person. Takes more time, but most of these people won't answer the phone if they don't know the number. Some may not want to talk to cops. Cops weren't always on our side... when I say 'our side,' I mean foster kids."

"Well, then there's me. I'm not a cop."

"True." She seemed to realize, maybe for the first time, that I could actually be an asset because I wasn't law enforcement.

"Okay, so we have twenty-three other names," I said. "That's a lot, but doable."

"I can't give you access to our systems, but I might be able to get research to help."

"I have systems I'm allowed to access as a private investigator," I reminded her.

"Right. Do you have your laptop?"

From my backpack, I pulled out my laptop. "Here, I'll take these thirteen, you take the rest. Once we're done, we'll put together a list and start pounding pavement."

She nodded, the irritation in her posture loosening just a fraction. Perhaps the morning's moodiness was simply lack of sleep and not enough healthy food.

∼

A FEW HOURS LATER, we had the former foster children sorted into four piles: those with last known addresses, those we believed to be living on the streets, those living out of state, and those whose locations were unknown. "That's about twenty local we can try to talk to. The ones on the streets will be trickier. Out-of-state goes to the bottom of the pile," I said.

"Agreed." Kate glanced at the wall clock. "If we head out now, we might be able to put a dent in this list."

"You know, I could call some people from my team. Get them to go and ask questions, if they learn something useful we can go back and get official statements."

Kate hesitated, then gave me a look that said she didn't want help but knew she needed it. Pressing further, I said, "He's going to kill again." My assumption was the killer was a male. There weren't many women with enough strength to shove a body up a chimney, but it was possible.

"If you want to bring in a few people just to ask questions, that's fine. The ones on the street are tough to talk to. Is there anyone good at approaching them?"

"I've got a few. They're younger, but they can handle themselves."

"Those neighborhoods aren't particularly safe for anyone walking around asking questions."

My thoughts drifted to Selena again. She often thought she was invincible, but she wasn't. "They'll go in pairs. Why don't you and I hit the first ones together? Then I'll see who from my team's available. We'll start small, one extra team, and see how much ground we cover."

"Sounds like a plan."

"Actually..." I realized it might be easier than trying to find all of them. "On second thought, we should start with the individuals with addresses. The person who did these crimes was organized with some financial means. They probably aren't living on the streets."

Kate seemed to think this over.

I continued, "Think about it. They've planned both murders, obtained drugs, and cleaned up crime scenes. Not that cleaning a crime scene would be a difficult thing to learn. All you have to do is listen to a true crime podcast or watch a TikTok video on how to not leave evidence behind, but they had to have some means. That Santa suit looked expensive. Maybe not rich, but not broke either."

"You're right. Let's focus on the names with addresses first."

It was almost lunchtime. "We could grab something quick to eat before heading out," I suggested.

Kate gave me a weary look, like she just wanted to start knocking on doors. But I could tell she could use some protein, maybe even a few vegetables. "Just a quick lunch to keep our strength up," I said. "Caffeine, too."

She eyed me, looking almost amused. "I'll drive."

14

HIM

From the shadow of the parking structure across the street, I watched them step out of the Oakland police station. Detective Kate Maddox moving with quick, clipped strides, Martina Monroe matching her pace, their voices too low for me to catch.

The December light was thin, the kind that made everything look washed out except her.

Martina.

So that's where you've been.

I smiled, leaning back against the cold concrete pillar. She wasn't hiding from me. She probably didn't even know I was watching. That was fine with me. Soon, she'd have the pieces I wanted her to find. And then she and Natalie would tell the world, whether they wanted to, or not.

15

NATALIE

Thinking back to drinks with Kate, I started wondering if I should write an article about past Christmas crimes. If readers couldn't get enough of the current ones, surely they'd like a creepy history lesson. The first article about the chimney murder had gone semi-viral. The second one went full-on viral. Now there was this whole new movement on TikTok about Christmas crimes. It was as if they were obsessed with dark holiday tales. It was morbid, and served no real purpose. Simply gruesome entertainment.

That made me think about how I could make my piece different. I could write a summary of a few Christmas crimes and then tie it into the triggers for such crimes relating to Christmas. The stress that led to a spike in violence, suicides, and death. Not to mention, we had two copycat murders right here in the Bay Area.

I needed to pitch it to my editor, Eli, to see if he'd be okay with an op-ed piece. Usually, my work was limited to reporting on local crime, not opinion on crime in general, although I often wove it in, which I think made my articles stand out a little more. *This is a good idea.* And who knows? Maybe it could even help Kate's case.

If I could do an article on crimes that happened around Christmas, maybe I could predict when, or if, there would be a next kill. Or maybe help prevent future crimes. There were only two murders so far, but was it possible we had a serial killer in our midst? Technically, we'd need one more murder for it to be considered a serial, but wouldn't that be something? A Christmas serial killer. Had there ever been one?

Curiosity got the better of me. I slid into my chair and woke up my computer, fingers tapping impatiently as the search engine loaded. I typed: *Has there ever been a Christmas serial killer?* And waited for the results to pop up.

People loved morbid stuff like this. I could already see the headline forming.

The search results loaded.

Yes. There had been killers linked to holiday murders, but as I skimmed the details, none of them were quite like this one. They weren't copying anybody. They were just straight-up psychopaths. I clicked on the first case.

The Santa Strangler, Adolph Laudenberg. He murdered at least three women, possibly as many as five, between December 25, 1972, and March 1975 in Los Angeles and San Francisco. His first known victim was killed on Christmas Day, strangled with a pair of pantyhose. The press latched onto the Christmas connection, even though his later murders weren't holiday-linked. Laudenberg was a retired merchant marine who targeted women he met in bars, often luring them to his home before killing them. He wasn't caught until decades later, when DNA linked him to the crimes.

Next there were the 1992 Dayton Christmas Killings. A spree, not a serial case, but still brutal. Between Christmas Eve and December 26th, four people, three men and a woman, went on a drug- and alcohol-fueled rampage in Dayton, Ohio. They carjacked, robbed, and murdered six people in total, including a convenience store clerk and a man delivering a Christmas gift. One victim was shot execution-style in front of his girlfriend.

Yikes.

Then there was the Santa Claus the Serial Killer, Bruce McArthur, in Toronto. Between 2010 and 2017, McArthur murdered at least eight men, most of them from Toronto's gay community. He buried their dismembered remains in planters at properties where he worked as a landscaper. His "Santa Claus" nickname came from the fact that he often played Santa at a local mall during the holidays with a full white beard, red suit... the whole shebang. The contrast between the wholesome image and the gruesome reality made international headlines.

None of these killers had tried to recreate famous holiday crimes. They killed for their own reasons. Which begged the question: Why copy?

If our Bay Area killer was a foster kid, as Kate and I suspected, then the trauma angle had to be considered. Studies showed that about 70% of serial killers reported experiencing abuse, neglect, or severe childhood trauma. Many grew up in unstable homes, and a disproportionate number spent time in the foster system. Not all trauma lead to violence, but in combination with certain personality traits, it could shape someone into a predator.

And then there was the so-called Macdonald Triad, the infamous "trifecta" profilers used to look for: cruelty to animals, persistent bedwetting beyond the normal age, and setting fires. Later research showed it wasn't a perfect predictor, but there was still a correlation, especially between animal cruelty and later violence.

Statistically, most serial killers were male, over 90%, with an average starting age in their late 20s to early 30s. Many escalated over time, their cooling-off periods shrinking as they got bolder. But copycats? That's a smaller, stranger breed. Their motive wasn't just to kill, but in some instances they intended to connect themselves to someone else's work, as a form of tribute. They saw the original killer as a hero of sorts. The thought made my stomach turn. In other cases, they copied to confuse the authorities. And in the truly sick, there were the fame seekers who wanted to out-kill the original to gain notoriety. So what was this new killer's deal?

Not that anyone should kill anyone, that wasn't cool, but why? What was the motive for Christmas themed deaths? Was the Christmas angle even relevant or was it just a way to confuse the cops?

Kate was working the case, and she was quite good at her job. She liked to work alone, but she'd mentioned there was also a private investigator helping her on the case, a Martina Monroe. I thought it was a bit odd.

As soon as I got home after dinner and drinks, I looked her up. Apparently Martina was one of the best. She'd been in the news a lot over the last twenty years, solving decades-old cases, working for the CoCo County Sheriff's Department. Cold cases. The kind of investigator who didn't let go once she bit down.

If anyone could catch this person, it would be her. Not that Kate wasn't up for the challenge. She had a pretty decent solve rate, certainly higher than the state's current rate.

You'd figure if Martina could solve a thirty-year-old case, surely a fresh one wouldn't be too hard, not with the technology we had now. DNA. Fingerprints. Surveillance cameras. With Martina's help, they'd surely catch this guy. I hoped it was soon.

I nearly jumped out of my chair when Eli appeared at my cubicle.

"What's up?" I said, a hand to my chest.

"Sorry to startle you," he said. "What's going on?"

I leaned back, folding my arms. "Well... you saw how those first two Christmas crimes went viral. I was thinking... what if I wrote an op-ed piece? In the first article, I linked the murder to a copycat. Then the second one, also a copycat. What if I did something broader? A piece about Christmas crimes, detail a few of the more notable ones that happened on Christmas or Christmas Eve. Could be interesting, right?"

"Good idea. Readers would probably eat that up. If your other two went viral, this one probably would too. People love seeing the not-so-shiny side of Christmas. We can make room for it. Can you have it done in the next couple of days?"

"Of course. In plenty of time for Christmas."

"Good."

With a satisfied smile, I turned back to my monitor. "Was there something you wanted?"

"Just seeing if you've got any new leads on the two Christmas crimes."

"Not yet. I went out with Kate last night, but all I know is she's got a private investigator working with her now."

"Really?"

"Some hotshot named Martina Monroe."

"Of Drakos Monroe Security & Investigations?"

"You've heard of them?"

"Oh yeah. I wonder why she's working on it."

"Kate didn't say."

Eli scratched his chin, his 5 o'clock shadow on full display. "Interesting. See if you can get Kate to tell you why Martina's involved."

"Will do."

"Keep up the good work, Natalie."

I smiled faintly. I didn't get a lot of praise from Eli. He wasn't a bad boss, but his feedback was more the no-news-is-good-news kind of praise. If he wasn't telling me I was doing a bad job, it meant I was doing a good one. Maybe the holiday season was making him a little jollier.

I returned to my computer, Christmas music playing softly in my ears. Taylor Swift's "Tis the Damn Season," filled my air pods, and I hummed along as I continued my research in order to start drafting my article.

That's when it popped up. A hit on a 2005 fire on Christmas Day. I clicked, and the article filled my screen. As I read the first few paragraphs, I gasped, my breath catching in my throat. This couldn't be a coincidence.

"Oh my gosh..." I whispered. The more I read, the more certain I became that not only did I need to write this piece, but even more importantly, I needed to call Kate.

16

DETECTIVE KATE MADDOX

As I stepped away from the car, the frigid air nipped at my skin. I took a moment to tighten my coat around me. We were about to approach the third name on our list when my phone buzzed. It was a call from Natalie. I hesitated, thumb hovering over the screen, and ignored the call. Whatever it was it could wait. Sliding the phone back into my pocket, I caught sight of Martina waiting at the curb, hands tucked into her coat pockets.

"Everything okay?" she asked.

She had a way of mothering people that I wasn't sure everyone appreciated. Maybe it got on some nerves. But she made sure I was eating, checking in on me, and noticing things others might ignore. Maybe she could sense that these interviews were scraping at old, painful memories.

"Yep, I'm just hoping we get a hold of at least one of them today. Any word from your team?"

"Not yet. Vincent is just about to head out to start on their list."

It must be nice to be the boss and have the authority to tell your team what to do.

With a nod, we moved toward the townhouse. It was in a well-kept neighborhood. It had beige siding with white trim, a neat lawn, and a few trees scattered in the yard. I wasn't sure if I believed Crystal Anderson really lived there.

At the front door, Martina knocked.

While we waited, she said, "Maybe I should ask the questions. It might come off less..." Her words trailed off.

"Official?" Her eyes met mine, and I reminded her, "But we need an official statement, and I should disclose that I'm a detective."

"You're right. You take the lead," she said.

I gave a short nod and knocked again. I understood her wanting to be involved. Someone, most likely the killer, had been putting Christmas cards in her mailbox, not even mailing them. Physically showing up to her house to slip them inside. If it were me, I'd want to investigate too. But this was still *my* case.

A puff of breath escaped into the cold air as the door cracked open. A woman with dark hair and dark-rimmed glasses peered out. "Can I help you?"

"Yes," I said, stepping forward, I could see she matched the DMV photo of Crystal Anderson. "Are you Crystal Anderson?"

She opened the door wider. "Yes."

"Hi, Crystal. My name is Detective Maddox, and this is a consultant working with the Oakland Police Department. We're investigating the death of a former foster parent of yours."

Her brow furrowed, then smoothed into something closer to recognition. "I read about Garrett Slade in the newspaper. Somebody finally got him, huh? It took long enough."

No love lost there. "You don't seem surprised he was murdered."

"No. I'm more surprised he lasted as long as he did."

"Sounds like he wasn't a great foster parent."

"Those are very far and few between."

Didn't I know it. "According to the official records, nobody ever made a complaint," I said. "He passed all of his home inspections with flying colors."

She shook her head with a look of disgust. "I'm sure he did."

"Would you mind if we come in and ask you a few questions about your time in the Slade home?"

She glanced back at her home, hesitated, then stepped back. "Sure."

We walked inside and she led us to a modest but comfortable living room. Martina and I took the sofa. Crystal sat across from us in an armchair. "So," Crystal said, her tone hardening, "what would you like to know about Garrett Slade and his *lovely wife*, Virginia?" She said "lovely wife" like the words were poison.

"What was it like, living with them?" I asked.

She wrinkled her forehead. "It was like the military, if your commanding officers were both control freaks. They were strict. He was in charge, always. He did whatever he wanted whenever he wanted to."

The way she said it, I understood the implication. "Did his wife know? Did she do the same?"

She exhaled. "She knew what he was doing to us. She didn't stop him, but, as far as I know, she didn't participate either."

I glanced at Martina. Her eyes were wide. "He sexually assaulted you? And other foster children?"

"Every chance he got," Crystal said flatly. "And it wasn't just the girls. He was sick. Really sick."

I chose my next words carefully. "We've reviewed all his home visits and complaint files. There was never a single report against him."

She laughed bitterly. "Of course not. He would've killed us if we had. And that wasn't his only threat. He told us he'd hurt someone else in the house if we even thought about talking. The only way out was to be too much of a problem, or to run away so they'd move you. Not that other homes were great, but he was one of the worst."

"Have you talked to or seen any of the other kids from that home since you left?"

"Nope. Once I got out, I didn't look back."

"You seem to be doing well for yourself. What do you do, if you don't mind me asking?"

"I was a waitress when I met my husband. I'd gotten clean by then. We got married, and I stayed home with our son. But he's in school now, so I've started a home business. I've got an Etsy shop." She gestured to a tray of handmade jewelry on the coffee table.

"That's great."

"Yeah. I didn't ever think my life would turn out like this. I have a nice home in a nice neighborhood."

"I didn't either," I told her.

She eyed me. "You're one of the rare ones too."

"There aren't many of us."

"So," she asked, "are you thinking one of his former foster kids killed him? Because that's what I think. Honestly? I'd applaud the person who did."

"Did you have anything to do with his murder?" I asked, though I already knew the answer.

She laughed. "If only. But no. Like I said, once I left that house, I never looked back."

"Do you recall anyone who got it worse than you? Someone who might've done this?"

"No one specific. But you've got his list of kids, right? Go down it. Someone might still hold a grudge. That stain doesn't wash off so easy."

I handed her my card. "If you think of anything else, call me."

"I will."

We thanked her and stepped back into the cold.

"Sounds like you were right," Martina said. "Somebody wants revenge."

"Yeah. Well, you know as well as I do just because a report says a predator is clean doesn't mean he is. It just means he hasn't been caught yet."

"Unfortunately."

Back in the car, my phone buzzed again. A text from Natalie.

I found something. Call me back.

What could she have found?

17

DETECTIVE KATE MADDOX

Part of me wanted to call Natalie back, but the other part wanted to keep knocking on doors, chasing down anyone who might know more about Garrett Slade. Curiosity got the better of me and I decided I'd call her back and see what she'd found. Inside the car, I glanced at Martina.

"Natalie, the reporter I was telling you about, she says she might've found something. I'm going to give her a call back. Is that cool?"

"That's cool," Martina said. She shifted in her seat, one hand drumming lightly against the dashboard, eyes on the windshield.

I called. "Hey, Natalie, what's going on?"

"Well," she began, her voice carrying that mix of excitement and hesitation reporters got when they're holding something big, "I'm writing an op-ed piece about different crimes that have happened on Christmas over the years, some of the more notorious cases, and I found one that gave me pause."

"What's the case?"

"Apparently, there was a deadly fire at midnight on

Christmas Eve in 2005 at a foster home in the Adams Point area of Oakland."

I sat up straighter, glancing at Martina. Her head turned slightly, eyes narrowing. "Really? My search hadn't gone back that far. That's something to look into."

"It's not just the location and the fact it was a foster home that is interesting," Natalie continued. "Two adults and three children died in the fire, but long story short, there was one surviving child who swears they don't have any memory of what happened that night and doesn't recall how the fire started, despite some whispers in the community."

My heart pounded. The surviving child could be our suspect. Perhaps exacting revenge on the twenty-year anniversary of the fire? But, if everyone died that night, who would they be getting revenge on? "Do you have the name of the surviving child?"

"Nope. Don't think it's a coincidence, though. The first crime, Garrett Slade, was killed in Oakland, a foster parent in the same area where the foster home fire happened in 2005. It was deemed arson, but the case was never solved."

"It is an angle, for sure. Thanks, Natalie."

"Also, I wanted you to know, the article is going live on our site tomorrow."

"What other crimes are on there?" I asked.

"Well, some of the bigger ones, some lesser-known ones. Nothing local. But do you think I should take out the Oakland foster home fire story in case it gives something away?"

And that was why I trusted Natalie. She had never done anything to jeopardize one of my cases. "That's a good question. Give me a second."

I lowered the phone and looked at Martina. She leaned back slightly, a crease deepening between her brows.

"Natalie's doing research for an article and she found a crime..." and I explained the details of the case.

Martina's gaze fixed on me. "That's a rather large coincidence."

"Exactly."

"Do we know who the child was? Where they are now?"

"No, but we can look it up."

"It seems like a promising lead."

"Well, the thing is, Natalie wants to run an article. She's putting together a piece on true Christmas crimes. I'm thinking we should hold it back. Or do we keep it in and see if it gets public attention? Maybe somebody will come forward."

"It's part of an article with other past crimes?"

I nodded.

"Maybe she should take it out. That way if we need it, she could run the story later to ask the public for help in finding a connection between the Oakland foster home fire and Garrett Slade. But I don't think we should run it until we learn who the child is and we get a chance to talk to them. We don't want to tip our hand if the surviving child turns out to be our killer."

Look at that. Martina was proving to be quite helpful. "Smart. I'll tell her."

Placing the phone back up to my ear, I kept my voice low and gave Natalie the update. When Natalie agreed to our plan, I exhaled and said, "Thanks."

"Any time. Did you find anything useful yet?" Natalie asked.

"Just that Garrett Slade was a creep."

"Figures. Dinner tonight? Drinks?"

"Sure. I'll text you later. I'm not sure how long we'll be out here. We still have a long list of people to interview."

"Okay, well, you can invite your *new friend* too," she teased.

I smiled faintly. "I'll talk to you later."

When the call ended, I sat back, debating. Inviting Martina

to a social gathering with Natalie could get messy. We were still figuring each other out. But Natalie had good instincts, and the three of us might be able to connect dots we hadn't seen yet. I'd wait and see how the rest of the day went.

To Martina, I said, "I'm going to call it in. We need to reopen the arson case and get the identity of the surviving child."

"How long will that take?"

A while. I'd need to submit an affidavit explaining why the identity of the child is critical to the latest killings. I could copy and paste the last one I put together and call over to the folks at CPS and then beg for a rush. "Hopefully not too long, but I'll need to head back to the office to write up the affidavit. But Tatum can get the case reopened."

"We could split up. You go back to the office, and I can talk to some of the names on the list."

"Or we hit a few more addresses, and then head back."

"And maybe by the time we're done, Vincent will have found us something useful too."

"Agreed."

Could this be the break we needed? The trigger being the symbolism of the Oakland fire's 20th anniversary. Most foster kids were in several homes. It was possible our survivor was in the fire and sent to at least one other home afterward. Perhaps they'd been one of Slade's victims. My chest tightened. We were getting closer, I could feel it. I just hoped we got to our killer before he struck again.

18

HIM

Sitting in my kitchen, the only glow coming from the laptop screen, I studied the photos. The smiling faces, arms draped around each other, mugs of hot cocoa clutched between them. The perfect picture of Christmas.

Perfect. *More like fake.*

The next message was already forming in my head. They were next on my list, and the list was getting shorter. I could picture their house, lights strung too neatly, wreath hanging just so, as if symmetry could hide the truth about who they really were. I knew when I'd strike. I knew how I'd get in. The rest was just execution.

A sharp thud at the door snapped me out of my thoughts. The newspaper. I rose, crossing the kitchen. I opened the door, glanced both ways down the hall before I bent over to grab it.

Inside, I flipped the pages. The headline hit me like a dare.

~

BLOOD ON THE MISTLETOE: THE DARK SIDE OF CHRISTMAS

By Natalie Sloane – The Bay Insider

Most people remember Christmas for twinkling lights, hot cocoa, and the kind of family togetherness Hallmark has made a fortune selling. But not everyone makes it through the holidays with memories wrapped in red ribbon. For some, the season's cheer is swallowed whole by violence, jealousy, and rage, leaving bloodstains where there should have been snow. Here are a few of the most notable, and most disturbing.

1929: The Lawson Family Massacre

On Christmas Day 1929, Germantown, N.C. farmer Charles Lawson shocked the nation when he slaughtered his wife, Fannie, and six of their seven children before taking his own life. Hours earlier, the family had gone into town for a rare treat—a new set of clothes and a formal portrait. That afternoon, Lawson gunned down two daughters outside, then murdered his wife and the remaining children inside their farmhouse, killing the youngest, a four-month-old baby. Only his eldest son, Arthur, survived, having been sent on an errand that morning. No one knows for certain why Lawson committed the killings. Theories range from a head injury to rumors of an incestuous relationship with his eldest daughter. In the weeks after, thousands of morbidly curious visitors descended on the crime scene, paying to tour the preserved home, complete with the family's Christmas cake still on the table, until the house was eventually demolished. The case remains one of the most infamous holiday tragedies in American history.

1945: The Sodder Children Disappearance

On Christmas Eve in 1945, tragedy struck in Fayetteville, W. Va., when a fire consumed the Sodder family home. George and Jennie Sodder escaped with four of their children, yet five vanished: Maurice (14), Martha (12), Louis (10), Jennie (8), and Betty (5). No remains were ever found, despite a blaze that should have left skeletal traces. In the days before the fire, strange incidents hinted at foul play. The family's ladder was moved from its usual spot, the house phone lines *were cut, and the truck George planned to use to flee wouldn't start. Convinced their children had been kidnapped, the Sodders launched a decades-long search. They erected a billboard along Route 16 offering a reward, received photographs of children who resembled their missing sons and daughters, and chased countless tips and sightings. Rumors swirled that the fire was set deliberately, possibly as retaliation for George's outspoken political views, and that the children had been taken as part of a wider plot. The case remains one of America's most enduring holiday mysteries.*

2007: The Denney Christmas Double Homicide

On Christmas Day 2007, the holiday calm in Locust Grove, Okla., was shattered when Jack and Elaine Denney were found shot to death in their home. The table was set, the holiday meal still warm on the stove, and wrapped gifts sat beneath the tree. There were no signs of forced entry or robbery, just the devastating reality that someone had executed the beloved couple in cold blood. Friends and neighbors described the Denneys as warm and generous, the kind of people who treated everyone like family. Despite a thorough investigation, the case went cold for more than a decade. Then, in 2018, a tip from a mental health professional reignited the search for answers. Detectives linked the murders to Justin Walker, who was already serving a federal sentence for unrelated crimes. In 2019, Walker pleaded guilty to two counts of second-degree murder and was sentenced to 40 years, to be served after his current term. For the Denney family, the conviction brought long-awaited closure, but the shadow of that Christmas Day will never fade from the town's memory.

2008: Covina Christmas Eve Massacre

On Christmas Eve 2008, in Covina, Calif., 45-year-old Bruce Pardo arrived at his former in-laws' home dressed as Santa Claus, where about 25 relatives and friends were gathered for a holiday party. Moments after being welcomed inside, he pulled out a semi-automatic handgun and began shooting, before unleashing a homemade flamethrower that ignited an inferno. Nine people were killed, several others wounded, and the home was reduced to ash within minutes. Pardo fled in a rental car, his Santa suit partially fused to his skin from the heat, and later died from a self-inflicted gunshot wound at a friend's house. Investigators uncovered that he had spent weeks methodically acquiring weapons, ammunition, and materials for the attack, driven by anger over a bitter divorce and financial disputes.

The Common Thread

From the Great Depression to the present day, the details change, but the pattern remains. The holidays have a way of magnifying emotions. Financial strain. Relationship collapse. Old grudges. And for a rare, dangerous few, those pressures don't just snap the thread—they cut it clean through. Fires, whether accidental or set, are especially cruel by erasing evidence, silencing witnesses, and leaving nothing behind but questions that may never be answered.

Breaking the Pattern

History has a way of repeating itself, unless we learn from it. Every one of these cases began long before the fatal moment. Long before the gun was loaded or the match was lit. They began with resentment that went unchecked, with isolation that deepened, with anger that no one challenged.

This Christmas, be present in more than just the gift-giving sense. Reach out to the friend who's gone quiet. Offer a meal, a couch, or just your company to someone who might otherwise spend the day alone. And when stress begins to boil over, step away, take a breath, and remember that no argument is worth a life.

Christmas is supposed to be the season of peace. We can't undo the tragedies that have already stained the holiday red, but we can decide, here and now, that it stops with us.

Because the best gift you can give anyone this year is simple: kindness.

And yet, call it a reporter's instinct, I can't shake the feeling that someone out there has already decided what they're going to unwrap this year isn't joy, but revenge. I hope I'm wrong. I hope next week's front page is filled with smiling families and stories of goodwill.

But in case I'm not wrong... I'll be watching.

～

When I finished reading, I leaned back, letting the words settle in. Slowly, I folded the article, smoothing the crease with my palm. I picked up a pen and circled Natalie's name, tracing each curve and line like I was committing it to muscle memory.

"She's watching," I said. "Good."

I took a sip of coffee as my eyes narrowed with a focus. Then, with a slow precision, I snipped the article from the page and pinned it to the board next to the others. If she wanted to watch, I'd give her something worth watching. My eyes drifted to the next photograph on the board, the couple with their perfect holiday smiles. *Soon*, I thought. *Very soon.*

19

DETECTIVE KATE MADDOX

Martina and I sat in our small conference room, its flickering fluorescent light casting a cold pall over the stack of case files between us. We were deep into the 2005 Oakland foster home fire files. The details were chilling, brutal enough to stick in your mind long after you stopped reading, and it was most definitely arson.

According to the reports, both parents had been tied up and shot. The three children were poisoned and then shot. The surviving nine-year-old was the only one untouched. No rope burns, no drugs in his system, and no smoke in his lungs. He hadn't been inside the home when the fire started. By the time flames consumed the house, all five victims were already dead.

The child's statement was strange, eerily so. He claimed he hadn't known about the fire until it was too late, that he'd been in the backyard waiting for Santa Claus to appear. But Santa never came. He said the sound of sirens was the first sign something was wrong. He ran around the side of the house to the front yard, where police detectives and firefighters found him.

The child never mentioned seeing anyone near the house. There was nothing in the reports to suggest investigators thought his story was suspicious, just that they had no leads, and the fire had destroyed nearly all the evidence except the grim confirmation of how the five had died. *It sure would be nice to get that CPS report on the surviving child.* I'd put in the request nearly twenty-four hours earlier. I had a feeling the kid could have answers we needed, but something told me he may not be our killer.

I turned to Martina. "You know, I'm starting to think the survivor may have some information for us. But how do you really go from surviving a fire to re-creating Christmas crimes?"

Martina leaned back, her arms folding tight across her chest, her eyes narrowing in thought. "Doesn't make sense to me either. If he was so traumatized by the fire, and went on to commit crimes to mark it, you'd think they'd be arson. Not something else entirely."

"That's what I was thinking too," I said, flipping through the crime scene photos. "But there was a fire set in the first crime scene. It was lit underneath Santa." I tapped the page. "Garrett Slade."

From the interviews we'd managed with a few former foster kids, Slade's reputation was clear. He was a predator, and everyone was glad he was dead. He and his wife, both. Martina's team had found the same thing. Alibis were still being checked, but most of them were solid.

Still, the unease in my gut didn't fade. We were on the right track, of that, I was sure. But something was missing. And until we found it, the whole thing felt like chasing smoke through a burning house.

"I agree, but I still think there's a connection," Martina said. "The murders started in Oakland, almost exactly twenty years after the foster home fire. That has to be significant."

"How do you mean?" I asked.

"The two Christmas cards I've received, from whom we

believe is the killer, they say they want me to show them, to show the truth. Maybe the suspect, in their mind, is a vigilante of sorts. Taking out people who wronged kids in the foster system. Maybe they want me to expose the atrocities against them. The bad actors, and the systemic issues within foster care. And maybe they knew about the fire. It could just be part of their message."

"So you think the message is that the foster care system is messed up?" I asked, almost incredulous. Not because I wasn't aware of how broken it was, but... maybe Martina was right.

"Maybe. And honestly, I still don't understand how I'm part of this, or why they chose to connect with me. The only thing I can think of is that I've uncovered a lot in my career, and I've unfortunately been in the newspaper more than I'd like. That's the only reason I can come up with. I don't even have any cases in recent history involving foster children or the system."

"You might be right then. Maybe he's just looking to you because he doesn't trust law enforcement. That would be consistent with someone who's been in foster care."

"It could be," Martina said slowly. "It could be that the survivor is the killer, but they didn't start the fire. Maybe someone else did. An accomplice. If the child had been involved, maybe now that he's an adult he has remorse, and wants to shine a light on how those kids were treated."

I cocked my head at her. "True, but if the surviving child was part of the crime, why kill the kids back then?"

"No idea. It's possible the killer had no affiliation with that family at all, and the survivor really was, for some reason, outside when it all happened. Or maybe he ran outside when the intruder arrived, was scared, and didn't want to admit that he'd hidden from the killer instead of going for help."

"That's a possibility. Either way, I sure would like to talk to the survivor."

Just then, my laptop pinged. I glanced at the screen and saw a new message.

"Finally. It's the reports from CPS on the identity of the child."

I opened my email. Martina scooted closer, her shoulder brushing mine as I read the file. The name stared back at me, one that could give us the answers we needed to solve the last two murders. Robert Flurry.

Apparently, Robert had been in the foster care system since he was three years old. His parents were addicts, and he'd been abandoned in a flophouse. From there, he bounced from foster home to foster home, cited for behavioral issues. And honestly, if you grew up like that, how did they expect you to behave, like an angel? Like you hadn't been dealt the worst hand possible?

In his teens, Robert ended up in a group home. He'd managed to stay out of legal trouble during that time, then simply disappeared out of the system. Nobody kept track of him.

I took a deep breath. "Well, we have a name. Now we just need to find out where he is."

Martina nodded, and I went into the database, pulling up DMV records. To my shock, I got a hit. I pointed to the screen. "Robert Flurry. 174 Brookwood Drive, Concord, California."

Martina glanced at her wristwatch. "We could be there in forty-five minutes. It's a weekday. He could be at work, or he could be at home. Or we could just take a look at the place. Maybe someone else there could tell us if he's still around, or where he works."

I looked at her and said, "I'll drive."

20

DETECTIVE KATE MADDOX

During the drive to Robert Flurry's home, Martina and I went over every possible scenario of how he could be connected to our murders. "He could be the perpetrator," Martina said. "He could know the perpetrator. Or… he could have nothing to do with it whatsoever."

"That's true, but he hits the profile I see of our killer. Late twenties, early thirties. Fit. If he has some financial means and a strong sense of right and wrong, it could be him."

"I agree with your assessment. But we should keep an open mind."

"Absolutely."

Martina glanced out at the passing holiday lights strung across shopfronts. "Only a week until Christmas, and I have a feeling our killer isn't done."

"I don't think so either. If he's commemorating Christmas crimes, there'd be multiple incidents leading right up to Christmas Day, and that's what I'm afraid of. There has to be something to tie our killer to these crimes. Unfortunately, I'm not sure we have enough data to do it yet. One foster home, a CPS worker, and an old fire isn't a lot to go on.

Especially without any physical evidence pointing to our suspect."

"I agree. But at the same time, it could be enough. The most logical suspect is a former foster child of Slade's. Or someone close to a former foster child of Slade's. Once we get a chance to talk to all the names on our list, get backgrounds and alibis checked, we could have all the answers we need."

"Or it was Robert Flurry."

"True."

"I hate having to wait for all of this to get done. Waiting is the worst part in any investigation."

Martina chuckled. "I agree. I'm not exactly known for my patience."

I glanced over at her, and we shared an unspoken kinship, a recognition of something we both carried.

Martina hesitated, then said, "So... Christmas is a week away. Do you have anyone you spend the holidays with?"

"Last year I spent it with Natalie. She doesn't have any family either, so we usually get together."

"Well, I'm having a big gathering at my house on Christmas Eve and on Christmas Day. You're more than welcome to join us, and so is Natalie. I'd like to meet her. She's a great writer. Did you read her article on all the different Christmas crimes, and her plea to the public to be kind to each other? She seems like a really special person."

"She is. Natalie always wants to do right by the victims. I think that's what bonds us. Well, that, and the fact that neither of us has family."

"Have you known her long?"

"About seven years. She's a bit younger. I met her right after she'd graduated from UC Berkeley."

"I see. Well, her article was compelling, and the fact that she connected the crimes our killer is copying is pretty insightful."

"It is. Honestly, sometimes we meet at a bar and go over scenarios for crimes I'm working on." I smiled faintly. "She's almost like a sister. But she's also one of those rare, truly good friends."

"That's nice," Martina said with a small smile of her own.

"I think we're here."

The navigation system pinged and I eased the car to the curb. We parked in front of a blue townhouse, its paint peeling in jagged flakes. From the property records, we knew it was a rental. Robert's DMV registration was ten years old, it was entirely possible he didn't even live here anymore.

We walked up the cracked concrete path to the front door. A faint smell of damp earth and dead leaves clung to the air. I knocked, and to my surprise, the door opened almost immediately.

Martina and I exchanged quick glances before focusing on the young woman standing in the doorway. "Can I help you?"

"Yes," I said, holding up my badge. "My name is Detective Maddox, and this is a consultant I'm working with, Miss Martina Monroe. Is Robert Flurry home?"

Her brow furrowed. "Who?"

"Robert Flurry," I repeated. "He listed this as his address. Does he live here?"

She shook her head, the movement slow, as if she were turning over the name in her mind and coming up blank. I pulled out my phone and brought up Robert's driver's license photo. It was at least a decade old, but he would still look roughly the same. He was young, with sharp features, and dark hair. I held it out to her. "Do you know this man?"

The woman studied the screen for a few moments. Then she shook her head again. "Never seen him before."

"How long have you lived here?" I asked.

"About two years."

"Well, thank you for your time."

"Sure. Good luck," she said, her voice already trailing off as she closed the door.

Martina and I headed back to the car. I leaned against the driver's side, arms crossed. Martina mirrored me on the other side, her gaze fixed on me. "If he's not here, where is he?"

"No employment records. No property records." I frowned. "It's... strange."

"Is it possible he's deceased?"

"You'd think it would've shown up somewhere. He has an active driver's license."

"Any cars registered to him?"

I shook my head. "No. Which is... odd."

"Did he ever?"

"I'd have to check the DMV records again, but nothing current."

Martina stepped closer. "He may be more difficult to find than we were expecting." She glanced around the street at the drawn curtains, the silent porches, and then back to me. "You know, finding people is what my firm does best. If we can locate him, it'll help the case. My firm can take it on. We have multiple people who can dig in. We need to find him sooner rather than later."

"I agree."

"Are you okay with my team handling it?"

I hated to admit it, but Martina had a way of getting things done with just the push of a button. "I'm okay with your team trying to find him. We could go the official route, but I've got a feeling your team's faster."

"I'll have my stepdaughter, Selena, do it," she said without hesitation. "She's a private investigator and has been working with our research team a lot lately. She'll drop everything to get started."

"Must be nice."

"Perks of the job," she said, already pulling out her phone.

After I'd met Martina, I looked deeper into her background, and if she said her firm would find Robert, I believed her. And I understood why the killer may have reached out to her to expose the faults in the foster care system. The way Martina had what seemed like unlimited resources made me wonder if I could do more good in a role like hers than as a homicide detective. I wasn't quite ready to admit it aloud, but I was beginning to see how lucky I was Martina had wanted to help with the case. With her, we might actually solve it in time for Christmas.

21

HIM

The table was set, silverware glinting in the dim light, as if waiting for hands that I knew would never touch them again. The holiday meal still warmed on the stove, the scent of roasted meat and cinnamon seeping into the air, clinging to the walls. Beneath the tree, wrapped gifts sat in neat little piles, their bows perfect and unbroken, tiny promises that would never be opened.

I let the scene imprint itself on my mind.

I thought, *Natalie is going to love this one.*

A calling card, if you will. Something just for her. She was watching me, and this... this would let her know I was watching her too.

The idea had been a gift in itself, really. My plan was unfolding exactly as I'd intended. And surely, with Martina Monroe working alongside Detective Kate Maddox, they would figure it out. But since they hadn't yet, I'd have to give them a few more clues. That was fine with me, it was already part of the plan.

Because the truth was, they got what they deserved. Too good for them, actually, considering what I knew. From what I'd understood, they'd earned every second of what I'd given them. I only wished I'd had more time with them.

Truth be told, at first, I didn't think I'd enjoy it. I'd only wanted to send my message. But I had come to understand there was a certain beauty in it. The final breath, shallow, and desperate. The widening eyes when they realized they were about to be extinguished. That moment when all the lies and bravado drained away and they saw nothing but me.

I wouldn't say I'd developed a taste for it, not yet. But I didn't dread it. I found a kind of pleasure in the process. The planning. The rules. The execution.

To be honest, I'd expected them to be more cautious about letting a stranger into their home, considering their own dark deeds. When you can't be trusted yourself, you tend to assume no one else can be either. But these people? They'd grown older. Softer. Weaker. Their edges worn down until there was nothing left but the hollow center.

A smile formed on my lips as I looked back at the scene. *We're almost there.*

Soon, it would all be crystal clear. Like looking into a snow globe. Sometimes you had to shake it, watch the flakes swirl in chaos, to truly see the picture inside. That's what I'd done. I was the snow. I was what they needed for the truth to become clear.

22

MARTINA

Lounging on the sofa in the living room, Barney curled up at my side, I cradled a steaming mocha with the peppermint sprinkles melting into whipped cream like little pink swirls. The scent of chocolate and mint filled the air, warm and comforting.

Selena sat across from me, her phone resting on her knee as she told me everything they were doing to try to find Robert Flurry.

"Are you getting closer?" I asked.

"I think so. Vincent is helping, but it's almost like Robert disappeared." She shook her head. "It's a little strange, to be honest. It could be that he's dead and maybe nobody's found his body yet."

"You think so?"

"Anything is possible, Martina. People aren't usually this difficult to find unless they're hiding from something or someone, they're dead, or they're purposefully living off the grid."

"You're right."

"Such a strange case," she said.

"I agree, I don't think I've dealt with anything quite like this before."

Selena scrunched up her face. "It's creepy. Like... the creepiest."

"I agree. I mean, the holidays are supposed to be filled with joy and love and peace and giving. But like the article said, there's a darker side to Christmas—higher rates of suicide, death, stress, mental health issues. A lot of feelings come up around the holidays."

I set my mug down on the coffee table and leaned forward. "How are you doing?"

Selena gave me that coy smile she always did when she knew I was prying into her personal life, the same one I gave her when the roles were reversed. "I'm doing okay."

"Are you going out with friends? Having some fun?"

She arched a brow. "Are you saying investigations aren't fun, Martina?"

"You can't just work, Selena. You know, I think you'd like Detective Maddox—Kate. She's a bit of a workaholic too."

"You're one to talk, Martina."

"I took the holidays off this year."

She raised her brows. "You're working an active murder case with the Oakland Police Department. Is that what you consider a vacation?"

"I guess you've got me there. I intended to take time off, but then the Christmas card showed up on my door, and I had to help. Plus, this creep was at our house. How can I *not* do something?"

Selena shook her head, a smile on her lips. "I'm not saying you shouldn't be working the case. I'm just pointing out that I'm not the only workaholic on this couch. In fact, the only one who actually relaxes around here is Barney."

Barney popped his head up at the sound of his name. I

reached down and scratched him between the ears. "Yes, Barney, you are a master at chilling out."

"You would have thought we would've learned something from him by now," Selena teased.

"You'd think. But not so far. At least I tried this year."

"I'll give you that, Martina. You tried. You tried to take the holidays off, but the investigation…"

"…found me."

"Yeah. Practically knocked on your front door." She paused. "How's Dad feeling about you working?"

"He's understanding, as he always is."

At the mention of his name, Charlie popped in from the kitchen, setting a plate of freshly baked scones smelling of cinnamon and brown sugar onto the coffee table. "A sample of the scones?" he offered.

"Yes, please," Selena said, grabbing one along with a napkin adorned with tiny Christmas trees.

I did the same. "Thank you."

"Do you have any more of those cookies your mom made?" Selena asked with a mouth full of scone.

"There might be a few left," Charlie said.

"When's she making another batch?"

I said, "She's having a cookie baking extravaganza on Tuesday, all of us are invited."

"I don't know about making cookies," Selena said with a grin, "but I'd definitely like to eat some."

"They're hard to resist. Plus, she said she'd make me some Christmas cupcakes too."

"Peanut butter and chocolate?"

I nodded.

"Awesome. It's so nice to have bakers in the family. Zoey flies in on Monday, right?"

"Yep, that's why the cookie party is Tuesday."

Zoey loved to bake with my mother. It will be so nice to have both my daughters home. It was just how I liked it.

Charlie plopped down on the loveseat. "You guys talking shop?"

"Just a little. We're still waiting on quite a few things, unfortunately."

"Well, Kim and August will be here soon, right?"

Hirsch and Kim were coming over for Saturday brunch. Charlie had been in the kitchen all morning. The scones were just a teaser for what was to come. He had cooked a huge brunch spread for all of us. He called it our "Christmas brunch," and I couldn't wait.

Having Selena there, along with my wonderful husband, made it perfect. Audrey, Hirsch's daughter, had a friend's party to go to, so she wouldn't be with us, but that was to be expected. She was at that teenage age where she was either sweet as pie... or spicy like cinnamon.

A knock at the door broke through the cozy hum of the room, sending Barney into full alert. He howled once, then leapt off the couch, claws clicking against the hardwood as he bounded toward the sound.

"Sounds like they're here," I said.

I picked up my coffee mug and headed toward the hallway, ready to greet them with a smile. "Merry Christ—"

The words faltered as I saw Hirsch's face, drawn, and tight. Kim standing beside him.

"What's wrong?"

"We're fine," Hirsch said, "but this was on your doorstep."

I glanced down at his hand. He held a red envelope, my name printed in block letters across the front. My heart rate kicked up as I took it from him.

I slid my finger under the flap and pulled out a card. The outside showed a snow globe, inside a winter scene, people ice skating on a frozen lake, a Christmas tree lit behind them, and snow falling all around. The pre-printed words read:

May your holiday be filled with cheer.

Beneath it, in block letters, was the message.

THEY DESERVE WHAT THEY GOT. TELL THEM THE TRUTH, MARTINA. THEY NEED TO KNOW.

At the bottom right corner, a small, hand-drawn snowflake.
"I need to call Kate," I said, already moving back toward the living room.

She answered right away. "Hey Martina."

"Was there another Christmas-themed murder?"

"No. Why? I mean... not that I know of. Why?"

"I just got another card," and I told her what it said.

"Shoot. Hold on. I've got another call coming in." Her voice dropped off the line.

I paced as I waited, my grip tightening on the phone.

When she came back, her tone was clipped. "Double homicide. Christmas themed. I have to go. I'll call you later."

"Okay. Let me know if you need my help."

The call ended. I looked at Hirsch, who gave me a slight nod.

"Sounds like brunch may be cut short?" Charlie asked.

"Well, there's nothing I can do right now, she's responding to a scene." We were expecting another murder, but this one felt different. What was different? I had received the card before Kate received the call about the murder. It didn't make sense. If there was no murder reported, how would I have tied it together?

Hirsch said, "What's wrong?"

"I've always gotten the cards after the murders were reported in the news. But I got this one before Kate was called to the scene."

Hirsch's jaw tightened. "He knows you're working with them."

I swallowed hard. "Does that mean he's been watching me?"

Hirsch's gaze held mine. "Why don't you, Selena, and I talk."

The warmth of the room had evaporated. The scones on the table, the smell of brunch from the kitchen, all of it seemed dimmer now, a holiday gathering soured by the arrival of a red envelope. It felt like Scrooge himself had just walked into our Christmas Brunch.

23

DETECTIVE KATE MADDOX

The house sat at the end of the block, its front yard lit up by the flashing lights of the police and emergency vehicles. I slowed my pace as something about Martina's phone call stuck under my skin. She'd received a card before I even got the call about another murder, *two* more murders. The killer didn't wait to give Martina the card after the crime was discovered, like he had with the first two murders. Why had he changed it up?

Did he know we were working together? How? As I continued toward the crime scene, I scanned the neighborhood and wondered if he was watching. Was he watching me? Her? Us? A knot tightened in my gut.

Approaching the officer stationed at the door, I let my gaze drift past him to the corners of the property. Before I could decide whether to walk the perimeter, a voice cut through my thoughts. "Maddox."

I turned toward the sound and groaned inwardly. *Great.* "Captain," I said, flashing my badge as I stepped past the officer.

The captain stood in the doorway, blocking the view inside. I continued, "I didn't know you'd be here."

Why was he there?

"It's a double homicide that we think is connected to your other two. It looks like we may have a serial killer on our hands."

"Well, if it's the same guy, then yes. A Christmas serial killer."

I studied him, wondering if he was there to check up on me. As one of the very few female detectives, it was basically me and one other among dozens of men. It often felt like some of them still operated in a 1960s time warp, the kind where you could call your secretary in for a cigarette and a bourbon.

"You didn't think it was important to tell me?"

"What do you mean 'tell you'? I just got here."

"I've been looking at your notes from the other two cases," he said. "I would've liked to know about the Christmas cards being sent to Martina Monroe. This guy's got an agenda."

"That's what we think. I told Tatum, and he approved us working with Martina. She's offering her services pro bono because this killer contacted her."

"I don't like this at all, Maddox. I think we need to pull other detectives to help you out."

I knew what that meant. "Martina and I've got it covered."

"Do you? Because there are two dead people in there who might disagree with you."

Heat rose up my neck. This was outrageous. We'd made real progress since the first crime scene. "Did you see my notes about the foster fire from 2005? The one on Christmas Eve?"

"Don't get me wrong, I see you've made headway, but I think it needs more hands. I'm going to bring in two of our best."

Groan. "Like who?"

"I was thinking Gray and Rodriguez."

"Okay," I said through gritted teeth. "I'm happy to work with them."

He gave me a pointed look. "They've got fifteen years on you."

"It's my case."

"Respectfully, it's my department. And if I want to assign Gray and Rodriguez and have them take lead, I'll do that."

I shook my head. "I can't believe you're doing this. I've been working the case day and night, and so has Martina. We're the ones making the connections. There is no one who knows more about this case than the two of us."

"Your reporter friend, Natalie, seems to know quite a bit too. She's been writing about the crimes in the Bay Insider."

"She has been finding the connections to older crimes. It's true. But she doesn't know all the details. She doesn't know about the cards to Martina."

I kept my expression neutral, but inside, I was fuming. Was he really planning to swoop in and take the case? More murders weren't a surprise. The only surprise so far was that Martina had gotten a card before I even got the notification. "Sir," I said, "I'm happy to accept help from Gray and Rodriguez, but I think I should remain lead. We can use more people. We have a huge list of potential suspects we're still going through, although Martina's team is making good progress on alibis and backgrounds. We strongly believe there's a foster child out there seeking revenge." I paused and tried to read his expression. He was stone faced, as usual. I continued, "What do you know about our victims in there?"

"James and Julie Stamford. We're running their backgrounds now to see if they were in the foster system too."

Without me? That was *my* job. "And it's Christmas-themed?"

"It is." He paused, then said, "Look, I'll keep you as lead for now. I'll see how Gray and Rodriguez can help, but I want daily briefings. I want to know what's going on every step of the way. We can't have a serial killer on the loose a week before Christmas."

Too late. "That's what Martina and I are trying to prevent. But

I agree, we could use a few more hands. There are a lot of angles to work. The suspect has yet to leave any usable physical evidence. But then again, the lab *has* been backed up."

The lab was always backed up, results from testing take a day to two weeks. As it was, we were still waiting on our team to look into the Santa suit. It looked unique, and expensive. Where did he buy it? There were no usable fingerprints or DNA left behind. Fibers could take weeks or months to process if it didn't get prioritized.

The captain pursed his lips, his eyes locking on mine. "I'll make sure your cases get priority with the lab. After you're done here, meet me back at the station. I want a meeting with Gray, Rodriguez, Martina Monroe, and Tatum."

"Okay."

"I'll leave you to it. I'll let Tatum and the detectives know what's going on. You can handle inviting Martina?"

"Will do," I said, summoning every ounce of control not to shout that I was more than capable of solving this case. After a brief goodbye, I shook my head and stepped into the home, following the narrow hallway.

On the right, a powder room. Beyond that, the living room. A Christmas tree twinkling, fireplace with stockings hung neatly from the mantel. The scent of pine and turkey and something faintly metallic hung in the air. I turned right into the dining room and let out a slow breath.

Propped in two chairs at the dining table were the victims, one male, and one female. The male victim wore a Santa hat. The table was perfectly set with red placemats and silver chargers, flameless candles still flickering in crystal holders. A beautiful poinsettia centerpiece sat in the middle, its bright red petals vivid against the white linen. The mingled scents of roasted meat, rich gravy, and the unmistakable scent of death filled my nose, turning my stomach.

"Hey, Dr. Lang," I said quietly.

"I think your friend is back."

He certainly wasn't my friend. "I see that. What's your take?"

"So, far, I've found a single gunshot to his head," she said, then glanced toward the female victim. "Same with her."

"How long have they been dead?"

"My guess is about eight to twelve hours. They were placed here shortly after death, or at the time of death and posed. They're in full rigor mortis."

That meant they were stiffly sitting at the table, frozen in time. "Did our suspect leave us any letters or mementos?"

"Not that I've seen, but I just arrived. You can ask Jeff."

Glancing to the right I saw the open kitchen where crime scene techs moved methodically through the room, snapping photographs and collecting evidence. I left the dining room and stepped toward them and said, "Hey Jeff, what did you guys find in here?"

"Mashed potatoes and turkey on the stove. Rolls and a green bean casserole in the oven."

"Who called it in?"

"Anonymous tip."

"That doesn't make sense."

"Why not?"

"They were obviously making some sort of feast. And it wasn't just for the two of them."

I frowned. The other crime scenes had been horrific, this one was no exception, but there was something ritualistic here. The victims posed at a table set for Christmas. The Santa hat carefully placed on the man's head, whether before or after death, pointed to a twisted mind. This wasn't just revenge. This was personal, and sick.

I walked back to the dining room, studying the wounds again. "Can we get bullet fragments?" I asked.

"I don't see an exit wound. Once I get them on the table, we'll get you the bullet, if they're in good shape."

A bullet could be useful evidence. If we could get a make on the gun and match it to someone on our list with a registered weapon, it could be the literal smoking gun. It was a small lead, but it was something. A clue, *finally*. Unfortunately, it had come at the cost of two more lives. My gut told me they'd once been foster parents, bad ones, or had worked within child protective services. If not, we had no clue what we were dealing with, and then the captain would certainly take the case away from me. I exhaled and turned toward the exit.

My phone vibrated in my hand. It was Natalie. "Hey, Natalie. Did you hear about the double homicide?"

"What? Huh. No, not yet. I need to see you."

"What's wrong?"

"Nothing. It's just better if I show you. Can you come by my apartment?"

"Yeah. I'll head there now." I ended the call, unease prickling at my skin. I paused, glancing back at the table, the untouched meal, the neatly wrapped gifts under the tree. My thoughts shifted to Natalie and her last article. I went to my email app and opened the draft she sent me. As I read the piece, "Blood on the Mistletoe: The Dark Side of Christmas," I stopped on one of the stories. My pulse raced. There it was.

2007: The Denney Christmas Double Homicide

On Christmas Day 2007, the holiday calm in Locust Grove, Okla., was shattered when Jack and Elaine Denney were found shot to death in their home. The table was set, the holiday meal still warm on the stove, and wrapped gifts sat beneath the tree.

My breath seized. He'd recreated one of the crimes Natalie wrote about. Was it a coincidence? Or was he following Natalie's articles and wanted us to know?

24

DETECTIVE KATE MADDOX

The road curved gently before dropping into a pocket of trees. The apartment complex came into view, crouched low against a strip of redwood trees. The ground beneath was carpeted in damp leaves, the kind that muffled footsteps. I slowed, my eyes tracking the gaps between the trunks. There were a dozen places someone could stand unseen, watching. Too close to the building. Too easy for someone to slip out of sight the moment you let your guard down.

I parked in the closest stall to Natalie's apartment. The twelve-unit building sat tucked against a strip of trees, the branches swaying in the breeze just over the hill, close enough to muffle the noise from the gritty streets of Oakland.

Stepping out, I scanned the lot. Empty. Too quiet. Even the usual hum of traffic felt distant. Something was wrong. I could feel it in my chest. I took the path to her first-floor apartment, my steps quickening. When I knocked, my gaze dropped automatically to the doormat's usual spot. Instead of the faded "Welcome" lettering, there was only a faint outline in the dirt, where the mat had once been.

Natalie opened the door almost instantly. "I'm so glad you're here."

"What is it?"

"Come in."

Her apartment was as neat as I remembered, every surface clear, every chair aligned just so. But on the dining table sat her missing welcome mat. At its center rested a snow globe.

"That was on my doorstep this morning."

I moved closer to inspect it.

"I didn't touch it in case it's evidence."

"Why would it be evidence?"

She nodded toward the base. "Look. On the edge."

Leaning in, I spotted it. Dark brownish smears in what looked like a star or snowflake design. "When did you find it?"

"I went out for a run about an hour ago. That's when I saw it. Do you think someone's been reading my articles and trying to freak me out?"

"It's possible." My chest tightened. "Has anything out of the ordinary happened this morning?"

Natalie shook her head.

Someone creeped up to Natalie's door and set down what looked like a bloody snow globe and then vanished. Who would do that? A psychotic killer, maybe?

I pulled out my phone and texted Martina.

> What image is on this morning's Christmas card?

Her reply came fast, a single photo of the card. The cover of the card showed a snow globe.

Not good.

I texted back.

> Thanks. See you at the station in an hour?

She responded.

> I'll be there.

Sliding my phone away, I met Natalie's eyes. "You were smart not to touch it."

"What do you think it means?"

"It could be a prank from some kid, or there is a possibility it's related to this morning's double homicide."

She protectively wrapped her arms across her chest. "Do you think it was the Christmas killer?"

We hadn't given our killer a nickname, but if it's the same perpetrator for all three Christmas-themed killings, we had a serial killer. The press loved to give them a nickname. "Is that what you're calling him?"

"It fits."

"We think it's the same suspect. The scene was Christmasy. Actually, it was likely a copycat of one of the stories from your article. The Denney double murder."

Natalie blanched. Her blue eyes widened. "Do you think he read my article?"

It was a distinct possibility. "I don't know."

Natalie began pacing and then a few moments later she said, "He is. He's reading my articles. This is a message. In the 'Blood on the Mistletoe' article I ended it with, 'I'll be watching.' This is him telling me that he's watching me too!" Tears began to fall. "This is bad!"

I led Natalie over to the sofa and sat her down. She wiped her eyes with the back of her hands as I tried to calm her. "We don't know that he is watching you, or reading your articles. This could be some kids pulling a prank. We don't know if you're in danger. But in the event you are, I will protect you."

"How?"

I wasn't entirely sure. "You can stay with me until all of this is sorted out."

Natalie wrinkled her nose. My apartment wasn't nearly as nice as hers. "Or I can stay with you. But I didn't see any security cameras outside."

"There aren't any."

"Or you can stay at a hotel, and I'll check in with you until this is over and we catch this guy."

She eyed me. "I thought you were going to tell me I was overreacting. Not that I should go into hiding. Now I'm more freaked out."

That wasn't my intention. I just wanted to keep her safe. Everything inside me told me Natalie was right, and this was a message from the killer. "I'm sorry, I don't mean to scare you, but there's something I didn't tell you about the cases. The reason we brought Martina Monroe onto the case was because she came to me, because she's been getting Christmas cards we think are from the killer."

Natalie's eyes widened. "So you do think this is from him?"

I nodded. "This morning, Martina found a card on her doorstep. The cover has a snow globe on it, just like this one. And he draws a snowflake inside the card."

In a quiet voice, she said, "The killer was at my doorstep."

Unfortunately, I believed that to be true. My mind raced trying to make sense of this, or how it could help us catch him. It wasn't likely we'd find fingerprints or DNA on the snow globe. There weren't any security cameras on her building... but there had to be traffic cameras nearby. There were likely traffic cameras surrounding Martina's neighborhood too. If we could find a common vehicle, we could find our killer.

25

HIM

Hidden behind the wide trunk of a redwood, I watched as Detective Kate Maddox and Natalie Sloane stepped out of her apartment. It was a busy morning for our detective. First, a crime scene. Now, rushing to the aid of her closest, and, as far as I could tell, only friend.

Oh, look at that. They're preserving evidence. Thoughtful Natalie hadn't touched it. She cradled the welcome mat in her hands, careful not to disturb the snow globe resting at its center. A gift. From me.

Did she realize it was from me? Did she feel me close, so close we could be breathing the same air? We were kindred spirits, she and I. She was watching me, and I was watching her.

My plan was working out better than I'd planned. They were probably headed to the station now. I chuckled under my breath. When I started this journey, to show the world what foster children had endured, I thought it might be difficult. *Risky.* That I might get caught. That I'd have to gamble everything just to tell the story. But it was falling into place, as if the world wanted it to be told. Not that I had much to lose anymore.

A face flashed in my mind, frozen in time. Pale. Vacant eyes staring into nothing. She hadn't always looked like that. She'd been vibrant, and sharp, when she was clean. She could have been anything. But she'd been dealt a hand so bad it made you question the point of even trying.

I tried to help her. Paid for rehab. For school. Told her she wasn't like the others, that she could make it out. But her pain was too deep. Her demons were too big, too sharp-clawed. They sank into her and refused to let go. She told me she just wanted them gone.

I wondered, was she at peace? Or was she simply nothing?

Lately, as I encountered death, I'd wondered what happened when we go. Heaven? Hell? Or just an end and we fade into nothingness?

When I found her that day, I felt gutted. Like the world had lost all meaning. But it also became clear I had to do something. I had to tell her story. Make them pay. People needed to know what they'd done.

And that's exactly what I was going to do. By any means necessary. The world would hear her story, and the stories of all the other children who'd suffered in their hands. I didn't want to hurt the innocent. But maybe it would be necessary, and I could live with that. Some sacrifices were justified when you're serving the greater good.

26

MARTINA

Stepping inside the police station, a chill went down my spine. It could be from the outside air still clinging to my skin, or something more ominous. I paused and glanced over my shoulder to look through the glass doors. Only a few people moved through the parking lot, some were uniformed officers, and others civilians, but no one appeared out of place or suspicious. I turned back toward the office and texted Kate.

I'm here.

As I waited, I thought about the events over the past week. Four murders, and three Christmas cards. For those involved, it wasn't a very merry Christmas. And I couldn't help but wonder who he would go after next.

The killer knew where I lived. I began to wonder if I should cancel Christmas altogether? We could always change venues and have Mom and Ted host instead, to keep this monster away from my loved ones. I didn't feel particularly threatened, but that didn't mean things couldn't turn in an instant. As far as I was concerned our suspect wasn't predictable. We didn't know enough about him, and that was worrisome.

My fingers tightened around my phone as if I could somehow keep the danger at bay through sheer grip. It seemed like the killer wanted my help, but from what I could tell, they were... unhinged. If they decided I wasn't helping enough, what was to stop them from coming after me or my family? I didn't like it. Not one bit.

Kate appeared, striding toward me with a young woman at her side. Kate's steps were brisk and her expression set in a look that warned me something was wrong. The woman beside her had dirty-blonde hair that framed her pale skin. Her blue eyes were sharp but wary, the kind that had seen too much.

"Hi, Kate."

"Hey," Kate said. "This is Natalie Sloane."

I reached out and shook her hand. "Nice to meet you."

"You too," she said quietly.

Kate motioned for us to step aside. The three of us huddled together in the corner near a bulletin board. She exhaled sharply, clearly annoyed about something. "I just wanted a minute to talk to you before we met with the others," she said. "My captain showed up at the crime scene this morning. He wants to bring in some more detectives. Gray, Rodriguez, and my lieutenant are going to sit in on the meeting. I think they're trying to take over the case."

"I think we could probably use some more people on this," I said. "Have you worked with them before?"

"Not directly. But they're seasoned detectives. The captain was insinuating they should take over, but I talked him out of it. I think we're doing a pretty good job, don't you?"

I did think we were doing a good job, but there had been four murders. There should be an entire team working this, not just one PI consultant with her firm and one detective. "I've worked with teams of detectives before. It could work to our advantage. We just have to play this right. They probably don't actually want to take the case away."

She gave me a look, clearly surprised by my answer.

"It'll work out," I said, adjusting my scarf. "Not to sound rude, but why is Natalie here?"

Kate's expression darkened. "That's because she got a gift this morning. On her doorstep."

Oh no. "What did she get on her doorstep?"

"What looks like a bloody snow globe."

The weight of the implication settled in my gut.

"I want to keep her here with us, to make sure she's safe," Kate said.

"That's smart. But maybe we should move her somewhere until we find the killer."

"I'm just trying to figure out the safest place for her."

Normally, I'd offer up my house, but the killer had been there too. "She could go to a hotel."

Natalie frowned. "So you're just gonna, like, sequester me? I'm a reporter, this could be a career-making story."

Natalie was younger than I was expecting. She had the pluck of Zoey and appeared to have a stubborn streak like Selena. "He's dangerous," I said, locking eyes with her.

Kate stepped in. "We don't have to decide anything right now. While we meet with the others, why don't you just hang out at my desk?"

Natalie rolled her eyes. "Okey-dokey."

Kate glanced over her shoulder, her expression tightening. A large man, about six feet five inches, wearing a captain's uniform, met her eyes briefly from across the bullpen before looking away. She turned back toward me, and said in a low voice, "They're waiting for us, Martina. We should go inside."

I nodded, then reached over and patted Natalie on the shoulder. "This is going to get worked out. You're going to be fine, okay?"

She gave me a quick nod. Her lips pressed together as though she had more to say but decided against it. Without a word, she followed us through the maze of cubicles, the hum of ringing phones and clattering keyboards filling the space. She slipped into Kate's desk chair while we continued down the hallway toward a closed conference room.

Kate opened the door and the muted buzz of the bullpen gave way to a quieter, more contained space. Inside, two gentlemen in their fifties, one in uniform, and one in a navy sport coat stood by the table. Their attention turned toward us. A third man, in his forties, leaned against the wall with his arms crossed.

Kate shut the door with a soft click. "Hello, everyone. I'd like to introduce you to Martina Monroe, if you don't already know her. This is Captain LaSalle, Detective Gray, Detective Rodriguez, and Lieutenant Tatum."

I lifted my hand in greeting.

"As all of you know, she's been helping on the case and I think you all know her reputation and understand we're lucky to have her here."

When I met Kate just a few days ago, she seemed quite skeptical of me, but it appeared she had decided I was an ally and an asset. *Good.*

The captain stepped forward and shook my hand firmly. "Ms. Monroe, it's very nice to meet you, and yes, I agree, we're lucky. Your reputation precedes you."

After a round of handshakes, the team sat as the captain remained standing at the head of the table, posture straight, hands clasped behind his back.

"So," he began, sweeping the room with a glance, "I wanted all of us together to be up to date on the cases. Kate will give us an outline of where we are right now, and then we'll divvy up some work. We can't have this guy—"

"The Christmas Killer," Kate cut in.

The captain shot her a look.

"That's what Natalie is calling him," she clarified.

He shrugged. "Fine. The Christmas Killer terrorizing the Bay Area. It's less than a week from Christmas. We need to catch this guy. Kate, why don't you tell us where we're at, what we're waiting for, and how you see us dividing the work to catch him as fast as possible. Our media liaison wants a press conference, so I need to know everything."

Kate stood and opened her laptop. The projector hummed and the first image was projected on the wall. The first crime scene. Garrett Slade, foster parent, dressed as Santa and shoved up the chimney. After a brief description and a run through of all the crime scene photos, she moved onto the next. Margaret Lawson, found in her bathtub surrounded by Christmas lights and a miniature tree. And finally, the crime scene from that morning. James and Julie Stamford, shot, then staged at their dining table. Presents stacked in the corner. Dinner still warm in the oven. The male wearing a Santa hat sat at the head of the table, as if waiting to be served.

It was extremely disturbing. "What do we know about James and Julie Stamford?" I asked.

Kate glanced at her notes. "We're still waiting on background, but initial searches show they were foster parents. The killer gave us another clue, a second list of foster children. We will need to cross-reference it with the first set of Slade foster kids and with Margaret Lawson's CPS files."

It would help us narrow down our suspect. The killer had provided us with seemingly helpful clues, hopefully enough to stop him.

Kate continued, "In addition, Martina received another

Christmas card this morning from the killer, and the reporter, Natalie Sloane, received a snow globe that appears to have blood in the shape of a snowflake on the rim. We'll need to have the blood tested to see if it matches any of our victims."

At first thought, we believed the suspect was seeking justice but these latest actions pointed to a highly unstable and deranged individual. That was *not* good news. Kate went on to explain all the information, autopsies, ballistics, traffic camera footage and lab reports we were waiting on, including Selena's search for Robert Flurry, the surviving victim of the 2005 Christmas foster care fire, as well as the priorities.

The room was silent for a beat, the weight of the sheer amount of work required pressing down like a heavy winter blanket. The faint click of the projector fan and the rustle of someone shifting in their chair were the only sounds. Kate was efficient, and I agreed with her approach, but it was a tremendous effort even for three detectives and a private investigator. Especially when the clock was ticking. There were five days until Christmas and I had the feeling our killer was not finished.

I shifted in my chair. "On top of that, there's another piece we should think about, and that's safety. I can take care of myself and I have full security at my home, but Natalie may be in danger. She's writing about these crimes, and he showed up at our front door and copied a crime she reported on. She may need protection."

Kate raised her brows. "If she'll take it."

"Well, I hope she will because her life could be on the line. I think the suspect contacted me to ask for help exposing the cracks in the foster care system. Why contact Natalie? He may want her to write a story for him. Which means he might contact her, which could quickly turn dangerous."

The captain nodded. "We could have her stay at a hotel and keep tabs on her."

"My firm has safe houses."

The group nodded in agreement.

Kate glanced around the table. "Okay, sounds good. Any questions?"

There were none.

"Excellent work, team," the captain said.

I turned to Kate. "Let's go talk to Natalie and get her situated."

"Agreed."

In my opinion, her life was more important than pulling records at this very moment. We needed to ensure she was safe. We walked out to Kate's desk. Her chair was empty.

"Where's Natalie?"

I glanced around the office. There was no sign of her. We walked toward the front of the office. No Natalie there either. "Maybe she's in the restroom," I said. "Why don't you text her?"

Kate tapped out a message, and we waited. And waited. Five minutes later, still nothing. No read receipt. No reply.

Kate raked her fingers through her hair. "Where is she?"

I didn't have an answer, and the silence from Kate's phone felt heavier with every passing second.

27

NATALIE

Fiercely focused on my latest article, I didn't even notice the time until my phone vibrated right off my desk. Writing had always been my escape. Once I started, the world could be burning to the ground around me and I wouldn't notice. I might only notice if the computer keys stopped clicking beneath my fingers. I bent over and picked up my phone. Oh, shoot. *Kate*. I should've let her know I was leaving, but I didn't want her to stop me. This was my career we were talking about, and we had basically just learned there was a serial killer in the Bay Area. A serial killer whose crime scenes looked like a merry Christmas. More like the darkest, most gruesome Christmases ever. This was huge news, and I was about to break the story.

Kate had texted multiple times, the last one was:

> Where are you? Call me ASAP!

I tapped out a reply.

> I'm at the office working on an article. Talk soon.

I hoped she wouldn't be too mad. I knew she and Martina wanted me in protective custody, watched over like a child. But I was safe inside my office building. There were other people here. Well, probably just the janitor. But the office had key card access and was quite difficult to break into. One time, on a weekend, I had forgotten my key card and failed to find a single easy point of entry. I had to go all the way home and get it. Plus, there were security cameras. I was safe as long as I was inside.

It was Saturday evening, and it was quiet. The faint hum of the vending machine in the corner was the only sound besides my typing. Earlier, I thought I heard a squeak of a chair, but when I turned to look there was nothing to be seen. Just a little old-fashioned paranoia.

Truth be told, it wasn't exactly bustling on any day. We were mostly an online paper, with a print edition kept alive more out of nostalgia than income. Last I heard, Eli said they were considering stopping circulation all together. Not enough subscribers, he'd told me. Either get rid of print or get rid of reporters.

I say, *see you later, print.*

I loved my job. I loved reporting on crimes, adding my narrative, letting the public know to be safe and be careful, and most of all be kind to each other. There were so many bad people and bad things out there. You'd think writing crime stories would be depressing, and sometimes it was, but there was always a silver lining.

Though this one, this Christmas serial killer, I wasn't sure what the silver lining was.

From what I'd gathered in brief conversations with Kate and Martina, they were linking the murders to the foster care system. My own research matched theirs. The first victim, a foster father. Second, a CPS worker. Third, foster parents. They must not have been good people. Which made me believe these deaths were some sort of revenge, a story the killer was trying to tell. Gruesome, highly staged scenes, like something out of a British crime drama.

The light above my desk flickered once, then steadied. My phone lit up again, this time, a call. With gritted teeth, I answered. "Hi Kate."

"You weren't supposed to leave the station. There is a serial killer out there, and he knows where you live."

"True, but I took an Uber. I'm fine. I'm in my office right now, looking out the window." My gaze drifted to the glass. The darkened reflection stared back at me, but for a split second I thought I saw a movement behind my own image. I blinked, and it was gone. "This place is like Fort Knox. I'm fine. Plus, I really need to get this article in. Eli's coming in tonight so we can get the latest news into the Sunday morning edition."

"We're picking you up as soon as we're done here. Don't leave the office building."

"I don't plan to. And if I get hungry, I can just order dinner. Not a big deal."

"It *is* a big deal, Natalie. You could be in danger."

"I'm safe right here," I reiterated. "I'm not planning on taking a midnight stroll to see if I can bump into any super crazies. I'll just be at my desk, typing away at this article."

"What are you planning to put in the article?"

"I'll report on the double homicide from this morning and connect it to the other two crimes."

"So you're going to tell the general public there's a serial killer?"

"Do you not want me to?"

"Not really, but even if you don't, the public will figure it out."

"I also plan to include my own research, that all the scenes have Christmas settings, that they're recreations of previous crimes. And I've done my own digging. I know all the victims are connected to the foster care system. This could be a vigilante."

Kate sighed. "Are you planning to include a message to the killer?"

"A message?"

"Well, in your last article you said you'd be watching, speaking directly to him. What are you going to say this time?"

A message to him would make for a great last line. "I haven't figured it out yet. But I'll send you a draft before it gets printed tomorrow."

"Don't include the cards and snow globe. We need to keep that quiet. And don't go anywhere until we get there to pick you up."

"Fine."

"I mean it, Natalie. Please, *please* don't go anywhere."

"I won't."

"All right. Keep your phone on. I want to be able to get hold of you."

"Okay. Thanks, Mom."

Kate let out another sigh. "Be safe."

"Thanks, Mom." I ended the call.

Kate was just looking out for me, and I knew that. Honestly, she was like a big sister in addition to being a good friend. She was overprotective, though. The kind of person who'd hear about a late-night hookup and tell me that guy could have murdered me. Like I was supposed to be afraid of every bump in the night.

I'd spent so much time consuming true crime, I probably knew better than anyone, serial killers were *rare*. I'd done the research, read the books. And because they were rare, this could be the story of my lifetime. The one I could write a book about after they caught him. I sat back in my chair. *Natalie Sloane, true crime author.* Wouldn't that be something?

A door slammed somewhere down the hall. I sat up straight. "Eli?" My voice echoed.

Nothing.

I shook my head. Probably just the heating vents blowing a door shut, it had happened before. Still, Kate had gotten in my head. I glanced around the office. I was alone, but Eli would be there in a few hours. Everything was going to be fine. I turned back to my screen, fingers resuming their place on the keyboard, and thought *Best-selling author Natalie Sloane*. That had a nice ring to it.

28

MARTINA

Times like these, I wished Vincent was here. Or Selena. But Selena was still trying to nail down where Robert Flurry had gone, I still wanted to talk to him. And truth be told, Vincent would jump at the chance, but he had a young family and it was important he be with them. Not to mention, I had volunteered for the gig. Kate, meanwhile, knowing that Natalie was safe and at her office writing an article and not kidnapped by a madman, was holed up with her tech team, digging through traffic cam footage.

Natalie made me nervous. She could have easily been grabbed from her rideshare. I knew that scenario far too well. I shivered at the memory.

Natalie needed to take this situation seriously. Not that I didn't understand her prioritizing her career, but didn't she have a laptop she could use in a safe location? She was young, and maybe a little too laissez-faire about this killer. After a quick prayer for her, I returned to my current duties.

I had the glamorous job of cross-referencing the foster child list from the Slade family with the one from the Stamford family, plus the client list of the second victim, a CPS worker. All I had to do was find some matches.

Tedious work for even young eyes, I thought as I pulled on my readers.

First up, the Slade foster child list. We'd already marked off the names of those who were deceased. Then I moved on to the Stamford list, using my own database to check for deaths so we could cross those names off too. So far, there had been five names from the Stamford list that were deceased. Five former foster children who had died. It was grim statistics, each one a story that ended far too soon. Something made me pause.

A familiar name on both lists of deceased. Linnea Porter. She obviously wasn't a suspect, but she was a common name between the two lists. The only common deceased name. I wrote it down in the off chance it had any significance.

An hour later, I was hunched over reviewing the lists, satisfied I'd been able to compile a list of names that were both foster children of the Slades and Stamfords. The last step would be to compare those to the CPS case list. Any matches could be our suspect.

My phone buzzed, and I answered right away. "Hey, Selena, how are you?"

"I'm doing all right. Dad wants to know if you're gonna be home for dinner?"

It was almost six o'clock. It had been a long day, and no one was stopping until we had a suspect, or at least a solid lead. But I did have a family, and sleep was always better than no sleep. I knew that firsthand. "Probably not," I said. "We've got some promising things to look through. Did you find anything on Robert Flurry?"

"Yeah, that's another reason I'm calling. I've been running death record searches, just to see if somehow he got overlooked or is a fresh body that hasn't been identified yet. So far, nothing.

So he's probably still alive. The only other angle I can work is that he's living off the grid or on the streets, but I don't think it's wise to search at night. So I'm gonna call it a day."

If Robert Flurry was living off the grid or on the streets, he wasn't likely to be our killer. Our suspect had a home, a place to do his planning. He had means to plan out the crimes. "Good. You're right, you shouldn't be out roaming the streets at night in drug-infested areas."

"I thought you'd think so. Anyhow, let me know if you want me to bring you any food. Dad's been cooking. You know how he is when he gets nervous, so there's plenty of food."

"I do know. No, that's okay. I'm sure Kate will want to order food in a little bit."

"How's everything going over there?"

"Pretty good."

"And how's working with this new detective?"

"At first, I don't think she was real keen on me being around, but I think we've come to an understanding. I've got her back, and it seems like she's got mine."

"Oh yeah? Why do you say that?"

"Because when more detectives were put on the case, she wanted to tell me about it first, to let me know she's afraid they're trying to take it away. She's putting me in her confidence... I feel like she could use a friend, you know?"

"You've already invited her to Christmas, haven't you?"

I smiled. "I did."

"Thought so."

"All right, well, you take care. I've got to keep going. Say 'hi' to your dad."

"Will do. Be safe."

I ended the call, feeling relieved Selena had been cautious, deciding not to go running around in the middle of the night looking for a potential killer on her own. Five years ago, I don't think she would have made that decision.

Back to my search. I continued to go through the lists. There were twelve names on both the Slade and Stamford foster child lists. I typed each into the computer, running them against the CPS case files.

Two hits. Three if I included Linnea Porter. The two other names were a Devon Kane and Marcus Farnsworth. My heart rate pulsing, I thought, *One of these two could be our killer.*

"All right, Devon," I mumbled to myself. "Let's learn all about you."

I tapped the keyboard. Devon Kane had a driver's license, a last known address, and some employment records, mostly in retail. His criminal record wasn't spotless, but it wasn't alarming either. He had a few misdemeanors and a couple of drug charges, but nothing recent. The last charge was more than two years ago.

Marcus Farnsworth, it's your turn. I found his DMV profile, his driver's license photo, his last known address, and his employment at a local landscaping company.

My adrenaline kicked in. Time to tell Kate I might have found our guy. I texted her the news.

Within a minute, she was back in the conference room.

"You found two?"

"Yes. And we have two addresses."

"Great!"

"Did you find anything on the traffic cams?"

"Not yet. Our tech team will keep going while we're out."

"All right, let's go. Do you want to tell Gray and Rodriguez?"

Kate gave me a look. "They're busy following up with family and friends of the victims. Trying to understand last days and activities. We can go."

She smiled.

There was no doubt Gray and Rodriguez would be more than happy to drop the task of talking to grieving loved ones to interview potential suspects. But Kate did not want to share her investigation with them. I was starting to see she was a bit of a lone wolf, one who didn't always play nice with others.

I grabbed my coat and bag from the back of the chair and prepared myself. Kate tapped out a message on her phone and glanced up at me. "Just checking in with Natalie." A buzz indicated a reply. Her gaze returned to the small screen. With a nod, she said, "She's fine. Let's go catch a killer," and charged out of the conference room.

I thought, *Yes, ma'am.*

29

MARTINA

I jogged to catch up with Kate. She was on a mission. It was no secret she was anxious to speak with Marcus Farnsworth, person of interest number one. I wasn't sure if she was more eager to talk to him or to get out of the police station before her colleagues noticed she'd slipped away to interview potential suspects. Either way, if getting a murderer off the streets was the end result, it didn't matter to me. What mattered was making sure no more bodies landed on our watch.

"What's the address?" Kate asked.

I read it off the sheet in my hand and she plugged it into her navigation system. "It'll take about twenty minutes, and it's seven o'clock now." She paused, then turned to look at me. "Do you need to go home?"

"Nope."

"You sure? You've got a family, people who are expecting you, right?"

"I spoke with my stepdaughter earlier. I told her I'd be late and not to expect me for dinner."

She tilted her head. "Dinner, huh?"

I grinned faintly. "I've got a protein bar in my backpack. Actually, two. If you're hungry."

Kate gave me a small smile, her eyes softening for the first time all day. "A woman after my own heart."

"Just let me know if you need it."

"Deal. Let's go."

We drove in silence.

Outside, the city lights bled into streaks across the windshield. I explained what I'd dug up on Marcus Farnsworth. "He's had a few drug charges like possession of crack, cocaine, and heroin. Nothing distribution-level, just caught with it. From what I found, he's currently working for a landscaping company. Not sure who he's living with. Could be living alone, or he could be living with family. He listed this address when he registered for employment benefits last year."

Kate's hands tightened on the wheel. "No violent offenses. Still, he could've been saving it all up for one big killing spree."

"True. But I was going through the CPS file they sent over. The file noted he'd been a quiet child who had been picked on a lot."

She gave a humorless laugh. "Yeah, and there's never been a story about kids who were bullied coming back for revenge, right?"

"Fair point."

She peeked over at me. "Are you wearing a vest?"

"No."

"I've got an extra in the trunk."

Glancing over at her again, I caught myself wondering if Kate was like me when I was younger. I was a bit of a risk taker and less inclined to play by the rules. Hirsch had called me reckless more than once and accused me of letting my emotions lead. Maybe he hadn't been wrong. Over the years, I'd mellowed some and learned to bend when I had to. But with Kate, I sensed she had yet to have a trusted friend in her ear to tell her that she needed to be careful, because her life mattered too.

"So," I asked carefully, "when you were in foster care was it common for the kids to be abused?"

She laughed, but it wasn't cheerful. It was short, with no trace of amusement. "Put it this way," she said finally, eyes fixed on the road. "If you landed in a home where nobody hit you, where they fed you regularly and you weren't starving, you were considered lucky. A lot of kids weren't."

Her voice dropped, quieter now. "Honestly, I *was* lucky. I only bounced around to three foster homes before I ended up in a group home. Sometimes I wonder how I made it out, how I didn't end up in jail or strung out on drugs. But I think it was because of the group home. The woman who ran it was an angel. Kind in a way most people aren't. She was there for us when nobody else wanted to be." She hesitated. "She was a former police officer herself. That's probably where I got the idea of going into law enforcement."

"Do you still keep in touch with her?"

"I did, until she passed two years ago. Cancer."

"I'm so sorry."

"Yeah," she said softly. "It was rough. But she made me believe there are good people in the world. As much as I see the bad, there are good ones out there. I'm sure you've seen it in your career too. Sometimes the good ones are just harder to find."

"When you do find them, you don't let them go."

She glanced over at me, then abruptly shifted gears. "So, what else do we know about Marcus?"

The change of subject caught me off guard. Maybe talking about her past was too painful. Maybe losing the woman who had guided her into this life, someone she was deeply grateful for, had cut pretty deep.

"Never been married," I answered. "No traffic tickets. Kinda under the radar."

She mumbled something I couldn't hear, and then we drove the rest of the way in silence. I felt a little guilty for bringing up something so raw, especially around the holidays.

"Right up there," I said as we pulled to the curb.

Kate nodded. We parked across the street from a house in Hayward. It was a mixed neighborhood. Some homes well-kept, others with peeling paint and boarded windows. One of those up-and-coming areas, maybe, but for now, it was a patchwork of care and neglect.

Parked, I headed for the back of the SUV, and Kate did the same. She handed me a vest, then slipped one over her head, pulling it tight against her body. I followed suit and then tugged my jacket on over it. The night was practically freezing, the only thing warming us was the adrenaline as we marched toward the residence of Marcus Farnsworth. The porch light was on. Good news for us.

Kate charged forward, every bit the lead, the one who liked to go in first. I recognized that fire, because I had it too. She knocked on the door. Three successive raps.

The door creaked open a few moments later. A tall man in his late twenties stood there, dark hair falling into his eyes, tan skin flushed with warmth, a sweatshirt and sweatpants hanging loose on his frame. Kate lifted her chin. "Good evening. Are you Marcus Farnsworth?"

"Yeah," he said, eyes narrowing. "Who's asking?"

Kate pulled out her badge. "Detective Kate Maddox, Oakland Police Department. I need to talk to you about a recent event."

His gaze flicked to me.

"May we come in?" I asked.

He hesitated, then shrugged. "I'll come out and talk to you. Give me a sec to grab a coat."

Kate and I exchanged a quick glance. My arm tingled as my hand rested on the weapon inside of my coat. I was ready to draw if I had to.

Marcus returned a moment later, bundled in a heavy parka. He stepped onto the porch, pulling the door shut behind him. Maybe he really had just wanted his coat. Or maybe he didn't want us inside for some reason. Either way, he could be armed under the puffy coat.

We kept a few feet of space, standing at ready angles, our stances unconsciously aligned.

"So," he said, folding his arms, "what's this about?"

Kate eyed Marcus. "We need to ask where you were last night between 10 p.m. and 6 a.m. this morning."

"I was here."

"Do you have anybody who can verify that?"

He shrugged. "My roommates were here," Marcus said, shifting his weight. "But sometimes they're drinking, you know? They might not have the best memories. Still, they should remember, we were just hanging around. Why? What's this about?"

"There was a homicide."

"Oh, dang. Really?" His eyes widened, though the reaction didn't seem entirely genuine.

I studied him carefully. He didn't fit the profile. His hair was unkempt, his sweatshirt and sweatpants stained and worn. He looked like he hadn't showered in days. No jewelry, no watch, and no signs of money, the kind of money you'd need to stage the elaborate crimes we'd been dealing with.

"Who died?"

"James and Julie Stamford, as well as Garrett Slade."

Marcus let out a short laugh, shaking his head. "I heard

about Slade. Good riddance. But the Stamfords too? Someone's cleaning house."

"Not a fan of the Stamfords or the Slades?" I asked.

"There's nothing to be fans of," he shot back. "Honestly, I'm surprised nobody whacked them earlier." His eyes sharpened. "Did they suffer?"

I kept my voice neutral. "It's unclear at this point. Do you know anybody who would want to harm the Stamfords or Mr. Slade?"

He snorted. "Whoever was in their homes, that's probably who. Shoot." He glanced over his shoulder, then back at us. "Truth is, I thought you were coming about Linnea."

Kate frowned. "Linnea?"

"Linnea Porter," he said.

My stomach tightened. Kate didn't know the name. I explained, "She was another foster kid that lived with both the Slades and the Stamfords. She died."

Marcus nodded. "Yeah. She was there the same time as me. We kept in touch for a while. But her boyfriend didn't want her hanging around us. She was trying to get clean. She was clean for a while, from what I heard. Then... well, getting clean's hard. I heard she OD'd last year."

Something didn't add up. "If she OD'd, why would you think we'd be asking about her death?"

He scrunched up his face. "I don't know. It was just weird. And her boyfriend was kind of weird too."

I exchanged a look with Kate. "Do you think her boyfriend had something to do with her death?"

"Wouldn't surprise me. He was real controlling. Didn't like her seeing us. Honestly, we didn't see her for a long time, and then she came by right before she died, looking to score." He raised both hands defensively. "Not that I do that. I don't do any kind of drugs."

"Calm down, sir," Kate said. "We're not here about drugs. We're here about homicide. We don't care about your habits. We just want to figure out who's behind all of this."

Marcus barked out a harsh laugh. "Why? So you can give them a medal? Those bastards got what they deserved. Just tell me where their graves are. I'd like to do a jig."

I glanced at Kate, uneasy. She leaned forward slightly. "We'll need to talk to your roommates, the ones who were home with you last night."

"Sure," Marcus said with a shrug. "I mean, they might be... how do I say... intoxicated a bit. But they're cool. I'll be right back."

He turned and slipped back inside, the door shutting behind him.

When Marcus disappeared inside, Kate shifted beside me. "What do you make of that?"

"I don't think he's our killer."

"Neither do I." She crossed her arms, exhaling slowly. "He doesn't seem sophisticated enough to pull this off. Like you said earlier, whoever did this is sharp. Intelligent. Psychotic, sure, but calculating. And they'd need means. Marcus doesn't fit any of that."

"Exactly," I said. "Still, let's check out his alibi."

"Agreed. We'll talk to his roommates, see what they say. Maybe keep an eye on him from a distance. But then we move on to the next name on the list."

"You got it."

After speaking with Marcus's roommates, who confirmed he'd been home all night, we had no choice but to believe them. As unreliable as a drunk witness could be, nothing pointed to Marcus as our suspect. We said our goodnights and headed back to the car.

Kate started the engine. "Let's head over to Devon Kane's

place. If it wasn't Marcus Farnsworth, then it has to be Devon Kane."

"Backup?" I asked.

She smirked, one eyebrow lifting. "You think we need backup?"

"I don't plan on getting shot tonight. You?"

Her mouth twitched. "I think we'll be fine. If anything looks dangerous, we'll call it in."

I wasn't reassured.

As she pulled away from the curb, I typed out a quick text to one of my guys, asking if he was available in case we needed backup. I wasn't about to put my life in Kate Maddox's hands. Not entirely. If Devon was our killer, it wouldn't be smart to go in without backup.

I was starting to see how she and Natalie got along. Both of them had a reckless streak. Natalie had walked out of the police station when her life could be in danger. Kate wasn't much different. Maybe we were being overcautious with Natalie, but the truth was, we were hunting a psychopath. And psychopaths had a way of turning up where you least expected them.

"All right," I mumbled, watching the dark streets roll past. "Let's go to Devon Kane's house."

Before we drove off, Kate's phone vibrated, she glanced at the screen. "The techs found something."

30

HIM

The reporter was burning the midnight oil, no doubt hammering out her next article about the latest double homicide. I wondered what she'd call me this time. A serial killer? A spree killer? The terms were always thrown around carelessly in the media, but I knew the difference. I'd studied them both. I had a feeling Natalie Sloane had as well. She probably knew that a spree killer struck quickly, moving from one victim to the next in a short burst of violence, often in multiple locations, no real pause in between. Messy. Chaotic. Like a wildfire that flares hot and burns itself out. Predictable in its unpredictability. And, in the end, usually forgettable.

A serial killer was different. A serial killer paced himself. He planned, calculated, and stalked. There was patience and artistry in it, a rhythm that only the clever ones could maintain. A serial killer didn't just lash out, he controlled the story, drew it out, and commanded attention with precision. I had studied them for years; every case I could get my hands on. Spree killers were nothing more than impulsive children throwing tantrums with guns or knives. They weren't in control.

But serial killers, they understood the need for control. They left puzzles. They demanded to be understood. There was something almost elegant about it. Sometimes, when I read about them, I caught myself smiling. Not that I was chasing notoriety. Not officially. I told myself it wasn't about labels, but if people whispered serial killer when they spoke of me... well, I wouldn't mind that either. Because I had a story. And I needed Natalie Sloane to write it.

I had no doubt Martina would eventually uncover the truth, the atrocities against foster children, the secrets buried deep. But I couldn't risk the police department sweeping it under the rug, burying the story like they always did. The public needed to know. *Everyone* needed to know.

It was only a few days until Christmas. Five days, to be exact. Four until Christmas Eve. Time was running out and Natalie needed to understand the narrative.

Natalie's cell phone number was easy to find, too easy. She really should take her personal safety more seriously. A young woman, getting into strangers' cars, flashing her location across social media, and walking alone at night. One wrong ride in an Uber and she could've vanished without a trace. Lucky for her, she made it to her office building. Lucky for me, too.

Natalie's image and information were everywhere. Social media was like a gold mine. Reporters like Natalie loved to be visible. Loved to get the scoop and send it out to the masses. That was useful knowledge. I called her number, but when she didn't answer, I followed up with a text.

> Hi Natalie. I have inside information about the recent murders. Can we meet?

I paused.
Waited.
Smiled when her reply came almost instantly.

> Who is this? When and Where?

I chuckled.

She was asking all the right questions, like the good crime reporter she was.

I responded.

> Your office tonight. Meet in the lobby.

Her reply came quickly.

> How will I know it's you?

I checked the clock. 7:30 PM. on a Saturday. How many people would be walking into her office building at that hour?

> Six feet tall. Dark hair. Blue eyes. Blue jeans. Black coat.

Another buzz.

> What should I call you?

Ah. That was the question, wasn't it? What name to give her? I typed.

> Dexter.

She didn't hesitate.

> What time, Dexter?

> 8 PM

> See you at 8.

> Perfect.

A face-to-face with Natalie. I would hand her everything she needed. The truth, with all its ugliness, and the proof of what those people had done. Who they hurt and why they didn't deserve to get away with it. Through her words, the world would finally see.

31

DETECTIVE KATE MADDOX

Still in the car across from Marcus's home, I immediately called the tech team back, and put it on speaker. Gideon was the one working through the traffic camera footage around both Martina's and Natalie's neighborhoods.

"Gideon, I'm here with Martina. You're on speaker. What did you find?"

"We picked up a vehicle that appeared around Martina's neighborhood earlier this morning," he said. "The same vehicle showed up near Natalie's place this morning. Martina and Natalie don't live anywhere near each other, so it doesn't make sense that the same car would be in both areas around the time we believe the Christmas card and the snow globe were dropped on their porches."

A pulse of adrenaline tightened my chest. "Did you get a license plate?"

"We did."

"An address? A name?"

"We've got both. Sending them to your cell now."

"What can you tell me about the name?"

"The car is registered to a Silas Mercer. Twenty-five-year-old male. No criminal record."

We hadn't heard or seen the name before. Who was Silas Mercer? "Thanks, Gideon."

"No problem. I'll send the details over now."

The call clicked off. Martina turned toward me. "What do you think of that?"

"I think it's strange," I said. "Is it possible our killer is working with this Silas Mercer?"

"I have no idea. The name hasn't come up anywhere. Not in the CPS reports, not in the foster kid files, and nothing I've come across."

"Let's go check it out. Where's the address?"

I scrolled through the text that had just buzzed onto my phone. "Looks like Orinda."

"Orinda?"

Our eyes met. Orinda was an affluent, quiet, and polished community. Not exactly the kind of place you'd expect a killer to call home. But then again, the worst monsters looked just like everyone else. Especially ones with financial means. "This could be him."

"Maybe we should call for backup."

I weighed the idea, heart beating faster. "Let's do a drive-by first. Check it out. If anything looks suspicious, we'll call for backup before we go in. Okay?"

She gave a tight nod. "All right. Let's go."

As I drove away from Marcus Farnsworth's home, the name Silas Mercer swirled in my thoughts.

32

DETECTIVE KATE MADDOX

After a quick text to Natalie letting her know we had one more place to go before I came to pick her up, she replied.

> No worries. I'll probably still need a few more hours to work on the article. Take your time :-)

Oh, to be young again, I thought.

Thirty minutes later, we pulled into Orinda Hills and parked in front of a two-story home. The neighborhood was quiet, tucked away among trees, the kind of place that screamed money and security. Christmas lights traced the trim of the house, glowing against the dark night. A tall evergreen in the yard was strung with ornaments and white lights, its reflection glimmering faintly on the windows. A wreath hung neatly on the front door.

It was peaceful. *Too peaceful.* "What do you think?"

Martina's eyes scanned the house. "I think we go in. If it's our killer, I doubt he has an arsenal. More likely he lives with his parents."

I agreed and studied the home again as we stepped out of

the car. The house sat quietly beneath a canopy of tall oaks and redwoods. The driveway was empty, lights glowed from inside. Someone was home. We walked cautiously toward the porch. My ears strained for anything out of place like shuffling in the bushes, an animal scurrying, or the shift of branches that might mean someone was watching. The wooded area around the house was thick, offering plenty of hiding spots.

The porch light flicked across our faces as we drew near. I knocked, then stepped back.

"Let's just play it calm," Martina said.

"Of course," I said, wondering if she thought I wasn't capable of calm.

The door opened. A man, about sixty, stood there. He wore a plaid button-down shirt tucked neatly into a pair of khakis. His expression was polite but wary. "May I help you?"

I glanced upward, noticing the corners of the porch had surveillance cameras mounted inside, one facing the driveway, and another angled toward the front door.

"Yes," I said, pulling out my badge. "My name is Detective Maddox, and this is my associate. We're looking for Silas Mercer."

The man's brow furrowed. "Silas isn't home."

"Do you know when he'll be back?"

"He's away at school right now. He's doing his residency in Oregon. He comes home tomorrow for the holidays."

"Are you his father?"

"Yes, I'm Ted Mercer. What is this about?"

"We believe Silas's car may have been involved in an incident," I explained. "Is his car here?"

Mr. Mercer cocked his head. "It should be in the garage. I can open it for you and you can take a look."

"I'd appreciate that."

The door closed, and moments later, we heard the low

rumble of a garage door opening. Martina leaned closer, her voice low. "Well, if Silas is in Oregon, then he's not the one putting bloody snow globes and Christmas cards on our doorsteps."

"If he's really in Oregon," I said. "Just because his father thinks so, doesn't mean it's true. We'll have the team confirm his alibi. In the meantime, we can ask who else has access to the car."

The garage lights flicked on. Inside, a three-car garage gleamed with order. Tools neatly hung on the walls, storage bins stacked against the back, and in the center bay, a dark blue Toyota Camry. The license plate was a match. That was Silas Mercer's car.

Martina and I exchanged a glance.

"This is his car," Mr. Mercer said before he walked around the vehicle and then patted the hood lightly. "I don't see any damage."

"Does anybody else have access to the vehicle?"

"Technically, yes. My wife and myself. But we don't typically drive his car. His brother might have, but I don't know why he would've done that. He has his own car."

"Does his brother live here?" I asked, leaning in.

"No. My other son, Caleb, lives in Oakland."

My stomach clenched. "Has Caleb been home to visit lately?"

"It's been a few weeks."

"Do you know if the vehicle has been driven in the last week or so?"

"I don't think so."

I tended to believe him, or at least believe that he believed it to be true. He seemed completely puzzled by our questions. "This vehicle was captured on a traffic camera," I said carefully.

"So somebody has driven it. Who has access to your garage? Are you home all the time?"

"Well, no. I go into the office Monday through Friday, and my wife also works. I can ask her if she drove the vehicle."

"Yes. If we could speak with her, we'd appreciate it."

"Of course, of course. Why don't you meet me in the front?"

We walked back toward the front door. Mr. Mercer opened it wide and gestured us in. "Please, come in. Can I offer you anything, maybe coffee or tea?"

"No, we're fine. Thank you very much."

The house was pristine, modern but warm. A fire glowed in the living room hearth. Stockings hung neatly over the mantel, and family portraits lined the walls. Two parents, and two boys that I assumed were Silas and Caleb.

A woman in a tracksuit appeared from the kitchen, wiping her hands on a towel. "What is this about?" she asked, brows knitting.

"This is Detective Maddox," Mr. Mercer said, motioning to me, "and her associate. Just some questions about Silas's car."

"Oh? What can we help you with? Can I get you something?"

"No, we're fine, ma'am." I stepped forward. "We'd like to know if you've driven Silas's vehicle. Or if someone else has driven it recently?"

She shook her head. "I haven't driven it. I don't think I've ever driven it, actually. That's Silas's car."

Mr. Mercer added, "I don't drive it either. And I don't think Caleb has."

I nodded slowly. "I noticed you have security cameras. Is there a way to see the footage to determine who's taken the vehicle?"

The woman blinked, then said, "That's an idea. Absolutely. You know, it's funny, our son insisted we install them, but I don't even know how to use the system. But I can get in touch with

Caleb and ask him how to access the footage. I can send it over to you. Do you have a business card?"

I handed one over. "Yes. We'd appreciate it as soon as possible."

"Of course. I'll call him right now." Mrs. Mercer pulled out her phone, dialed, and lifted it to her ear. The three of us stood in silence, the only sound the low crackle from the fireplace. Finally, she shook her head. "He's not answering. He may be out with friends. You know how young people are. Saturday night, he could be with a girl or just... out."

Committing Christmas-themed murders? "Okay. Well, you have my card. As soon as you're able to get that footage to me, I'd appreciate it."

"No problem. Anything we can do to help," Mr. Mercer said, ushering us back toward the door. Then, almost as an afterthought, he asked, "What kind of accident was this vehicle involved in? There's no damage."

"Oh, it wasn't exactly an accident," I said. "We believe the vehicle may have been involved in, or witnessed, a crime. Someone driving it may have seen something. We're just trying to get as much information as possible."

Mr. Mercer paled slightly but nodded. "All right. As soon as our son calls us back, we'll get you that footage."

Back in the car, Martina blew out a breath, her eyes locked on me. "I've got a feeling about this, Kate. Whoever drove that car could be our killer."

"Yeah," I said, tapping the wheel. "And it could be Silas or Caleb or Mr. Mercer himself. I have no idea how any of them may fit into the killings, but we'll also have the team pull additional traffic cams, to see if we can get a description of the driver."

"While they're doing that, we'll also need them to dig up everything we can on the Mercers."

"Agreed."

A silence stretched between us, likely each of us contemplating this new development. After a quick call to Tatum, I shifted into drive. "Now, let's see if we can find Devon Kane, and get some answers."

This latest development was puzzling. Was one of the Mercers and Devon working together?

33

DETECTIVE KATE MADDOX

Nobody was home at the address we had for Devon Kane. But something in my gut was gnawing at me as I sat in my SUV. Something I didn't understand.

"Let's call it," Martina said, rubbing at her temple. "We'll get Natalie and regroup tomorrow."

I nodded. But unease pricked at me. I pulled out my phone and shot Natalie a text.

> On our way. Be there in fifteen.

No response.

I stared at the screen, waiting for the little typing dots. Nothing.

"She's probably still buried in that article," Martina said, though her tone didn't convince me.

I hoped that was the situation, but something in my gut told me it wasn't. I prayed I was wrong.

The drive to Natalie's office felt longer than it should have. By the time we pulled up in front of the building, I sensed something was off. The lobby lights glowed faintly behind the glass doors, but the place looked deserted.

We hurried inside and I checked on my phone again for any messages from Natalie. There were none. The pit in my stomach hollowed out.

"Are you looking for Natalie?"

I turned to see Eli, her editor, stepping out of the elevator. We'd met a few times over the years at various social functions. He was gruff and not usually the picture of friendly. His coat was draped over one arm, his glasses slightly askew, like he'd been working late.

"She was supposed to be here," Eli said, frowning. "But when I got here, I couldn't find her anywhere."

"She's not upstairs in the office?"

He shook his head. "I looked everywhere."

My heart pounded in my ears. "Can you let us into the office?"

"Of course."

We followed him onto the elevator and when the doors dinged, we exited.

On the wall, he swiped his badge and the glass doors clicked open. The newsroom stretched out before us, two rows of desks, with darkened monitors. Only one desk had a lamp on. *Natalie's.* I hurried over and spotted her purse slung over the chair. I opened the purse and searched inside. Her phone was nowhere to be seen. Her laptop was gone too. I froze, staring at the empty space on the desk where her laptop should've been.

Martina whispered what I couldn't bring myself to say out loud. "She's not here."

The words rattled through me like a bullet. *Natalie was missing.*

34

NATALIE

With a gasp, I jolted awake, ripped from the grip of a terrible nightmare. My chest rose and fell in quick, uneven bursts as my thoughts scrambled for meaning. I blinked hard, my eyes adjusting to the dim glow of soft lamplight. Around me was what looked like a small apartment with modern furniture. It was neat, almost too neat. A stone fireplace, a dining table set for two, and in the corner, a medium-sized Christmas tree twinkled with warm white lights.

My mind tried desperately to piece everything together. How had I gotten here?

I stared at the tree, the blur of its ornaments sharpening as my memory returned. Sitting at my desk. Working on my article about the double homicide. That was last night. Was it still night? What time was it? Where was I?

Then the memory of the text came back to me, the anonymous source, the one who called himself Dexter. Why on earth had I agreed to meet someone with that name?

But I had. I remembered going down to the lobby of my office building, rationalizing it away. It didn't feel dangerous, there were security cameras everywhere. What could go wrong?

Then I saw him.

Dexter. Tall, dark hair, bright blue eyes. Handsome. Lean, with a trace of muscle under his fitted jacket. My first thought was my my my, he's gorgeous. But then, something changed. I reached to shake his hand. His grip was warm, and firm. That was the last thing I remembered before the world tilted and dissolved into black.

My stomach dropped.

Could he be the killer?

I'd done so much research on serial killers. I knew better than to trust appearances. Handsome or not, it didn't matter. They could still be psychos who chopped up bodies, shoved people up chimneys, staged murders at dinner tables, or did horrific things in bathtubs before decorating the scene like a twisted Christmas celebration.

Shivering, I adjusted myself on the sofa and patted my pockets. *Empty.* My phone was gone. My gaze moved back to the dining table. A laptop sat there. My laptop? Why would he keep that? And what had he done with my phone?

I pushed to my feet, knees trembling, the room tilting slightly. My head spun. A fog clung to me, heavy and disorienting. He must have drugged me, just like in the TV show Dexter.

How could I have been so foolish? *Seriously.* Why hadn't I told anyone I was meeting him?

If I survived this, I promised myself, it would be a lesson burned into my bones. Never meet a source without letting someone know where I was going. And next time, if there *was* a next time, I'd take Kate's advice and start carrying a stun gun. Or at least a retractable baton.

I steadied myself, heart hammering, and forced my legs to carry me to the dining table. The laptop looked identical to mine, the same scuffed model I dragged everywhere. I lifted the lid. Relief filled me. I could send a message for help. But the relief evaporated instantly. No Wi-Fi. I had no phone, and therefore, no hotspot.

My breath caught at the sudden sound of footsteps. I glanced up, fear rushing through me. Footsteps drew nearer. "You're awake. Excellent," he said with a smile.

Oh my God. He had kidnapped me, and now he was smiling at me as if this were a polite meeting over coffee. "What did you do to me? Where did you take me? Where's my phone?"

"Oh, Natalie." His tone was almost affectionate, but condescending. "You have so many questions, and I like that about you. I like the grit, and the tough questions. But let's not focus on that right now. I'm your anonymous source, and I'm going to make you famous."

Famous? *Famous for being killed by a serial killer? No, thank you.*

"Don't worry, Natalie. I just need you to write the story. That's why I have your laptop."

He was deranged. That much was clear. Likely psychotic, yes, but not without a purpose. My research had told me as much. He wasn't going after just anyone. Foster parents. CPS workers. People tied to the system. Maybe he'd been failed as a child, though looking at him now, he didn't fit the profile of most who survived that fate. He was clean-cut, groomed, and polished. The kind of man who blended in, who looked like he belonged anywhere. And that's what made him so dangerous.

He planned everything. The first murder was over a week ago, and he still hadn't been caught. No physical evidence, and no careless mistakes. He was meticulous. Smart. Far smarter than I'd been, considering I walked straight into his trap.

I forced my voice to be steady. "What story is that? What exactly do you want me to write?"

"Please, be at ease, Natalie." His grin widened. "I don't intend to hurt you. But I also don't intend to go to jail."

My chest tightened. "You've let me see your face. Of course you're going to kill me."

He shook his head, chuckling softly. "No, no, no, Natalie. All you have is my face." The sound of his laugh, too casual, too easy, shot a cold chill through me. He explained, "I can change the way I look, and I might. Honestly, I don't even look the way I did three weeks ago, before all this started. That's the beauty of planning."

I swallowed hard.

"They're getting closer, you know," he continued. "The police. I think they understand the foster child connection."

"Were you in foster care?"

He sat down in the chair across from me, his blue eyes unblinking. "No. That's not my story. But I do despise a negligent system that throws children to the wolves and doesn't bother to see if they're safe."

"So you're a vigilante?"

He shrugged, almost casually. "I really don't want to hurt the innocent. But those people weren't innocent, Natalie. You have to understand. You have to use your writing to explain it."

"What if I refuse?" My throat felt raw as I forced the question out.

His smile faded just slightly, replaced by something colder. "Why would you refuse? This is important. I can tell from your articles, you have heart. You have what it takes to tell the story the way it needs to be told."

"Okay," I said with hesitation. "And you don't plan to kill me?"

"I don't plan to do that," he said evenly. "So please, don't give me a reason to change my plan. I don't like when my plans change. Do you understand?"

I clenched my fists and nodded.

"Good."

The smile returned, and it was very unsettling. "Now," he said, leaning forward. "Where shall I begin?"

My stomach twisted and I braced myself for what would come next.

35

MARTINA

Kate looked like her head was about to explode. Understandably so. It looked like Natalie might have been taken. But we didn't have evidence of that. We had to keep our minds calm, though that was easier said than done when it came to a close friend or loved one. From what I understood, Kate didn't have many of those.

The man standing with us, presumably Natalie's editor, Eli, as Kate had referred to him, shifted nervously. I turned to him. "Are there security cameras in the building?"

"Yes, there are. Quite a few."

"Can we get access?"

"I'll have to call the building manager."

"Then call them. It's an emergency. We need to know if Natalie was taken or if she's just working at a coffee shop and not looking at her phone."

"I'll call right away." He hurried off, already fumbling for his phone.

I turned back to Kate. "We can't panic. We're going to find her. This could all be a big misunderstanding."

Kate shook her head, her eyes wide. "I don't think so."

"Well, remember earlier when we thought she was missing, but it turned out she was engrossed in her article and didn't see her messages?"

Kate didn't budge.

"She told you she wasn't going to leave the office building. But she also told us she'd stay at your desk, and she didn't. Instead, she took a rideshare back here. Maybe she's gone somewhere to grab a bite to eat."

"I don't think so. I think she could be in the hands of a killer," Kate said bluntly.

I glanced around the office space. Everything looked ordinary. Papers were stacked neatly, and chairs tucked under desks. "There's no sign of a struggle."

Kate raked her fingers through her hair as she stared down at Natalie's desk. "You're right. She left this office willingly, or with someone she trusted. The camera footage will tell us who."

"Does she have a boyfriend? Another close friend she might have gone to meet? A source?"

Kate's gaze wandered across the room. "She doesn't have a boyfriend. Nothing serious, anyway. She doesn't have many friends."

"There isn't much to go on until we get the building surveillance footage. Why don't we check in with the team and see if they've found anything new."

"You're right. I'll call and let them know we think Natalie might be missing."

I waited quietly as she phoned the team.

Her face reddened as she ended the call. "They just finished verifying that Silas was in Oregon, like his father said. And they haven't gotten the traffic cam footage yet, but they did verify Mr. And Mrs. Mercer's employment, but at this hour can't get a hold of anyone to determine if they've had an absence at work. They haven't looked into Caleb yet."

Suppressing my frustration, I pulled out my phone. "That leaves Caleb as our most likely driver. I'll call Selena. She's always working. Even when she's not, she's got her laptop and she's ready to dig right in. She can pull an address and background quickly on Caleb."

Kate gave a tight nod. "We have to find her."

"We will."

"You don't know that," Kate snapped.

"Look," I said, trying to keep my emotions in check. "I know this is the worst possible situation."

"Do you?"

"Yes, I do." My voice came out harder than I intended. "My daughter was kidnapped." I then told her the shortened version of the story, before saying, "So yes, Kate, I do know what this feels like. It's terrifying, and it makes you lose your mind. You make choices you normally wouldn't, out of stress and fear for someone you love. But I promise you this, when I say we're going to find Natalie, we *are* going to find her."

Kate's shoulders sagged just a fraction. She nodded, and I called Selena.

She answered almost immediately. "Martina, what's up?"

"Do you have your laptop?"

"Yes."

"Good. The reporter who's been writing about the murders may be missing."

"What can I do?"

"I need everything we can find on a Caleb Mercer. We believe he lives in Oakland."

"Got it. Address, phone number, criminal records?"

"Start with the address and phone number, and anything that'll help us. We think he may be the person who drove the vehicle that dropped those gifts on our doorsteps. We don't know for sure, but my gut tells me he's the lead we need to follow. If Natalie was abducted, finding him is our best chance at finding her."

Kate hovered nearby, flustered, pacing in short, tight circles. I didn't blame her.

"Okay," Selena said.

I heard the quick tapping of keys, and a few minutes later. "I've got a couple of addresses. One in Oakland, one in San Francisco, and one in Orinda."

"His parents live in Orinda. What can you tell me about the Oakland and San Francisco addresses?"

"Both appear to be apartment buildings."

"Tell me about the one in Oakland."

"It's in downtown. Pretty nice building."

"What's the parking situation?"

"Looks like it's got a parking garage down below."

"Okay. What about the San Francisco apartment?"

"Give me a minute..." I could hear Selena typing rapidly in the background. "It's also a nice building. Underground garage. He could easily park there and take someone up in the elevator."

A chill ran through me. "That makes sense." I stepped away from Kate so she couldn't hear me. "Another thing you might be able to help us with... if you can get access to traffic cams around The Bay Insider office building, it could help us see who she left with, and the vehicle that transported her. We're working on getting lobby camera footage from the building manager, but outside coverage could give us more, and OPD access to traffic cams is a little slow for my liking."

"Text me the address."

"Will do."

"I might have to call in Vincent for help."

"Call whoever you need to. And check, *quietly*, financials and do a wider background search beyond what would be in a police report. My guess is we won't find a criminal history."

"You got it."

I ended the call and quickly texted the address to Selena, my fingers moving faster than my thoughts. I stepped back over to Kate. "My team's on it," I said. "We have a couple of addresses for Caleb. One in Oakland, and one in San Francisco. We can decide which to check first."

"Oakland's closer," Kate said. "Let's start there. The building manager can call us once he gets the security footage." She glanced at her watch. "It's almost ten o'clock at night."

I nodded. "Sometimes you have to knock on doors at ten o'clock at night. And you know what? It's fine. I'm armed. You're armed. You ready?"

Before she could answer, Eli jogged toward us, his face pale. "I haven't been able to get ahold of the manager," he said. "I left a message, but I'll keep trying."

"Thank you. Call us if you hear back. We're heading out to start checking possible locations."

"I will."

"Here." I pulled a business card from my coat pocket and handed it to him. "Call me."

His eyes darted between us, anxiety radiating off him. "You're going to find her, right?"

"We're going to find her." I meant every word I'd told Eli and Kate. I wouldn't stop until we found Natalie and stopped this killer.

36

DETECTIVE KATE MADDOX

Fear gripped every part of me. It was a feeling I wasn't used to, and I didn't like it. There weren't many people I cared about in this world the way I cared about Natalie. She was like a little sister, someone I was meant to protect. Someone I should have protected. I didn't know what I would do if she wasn't safe.

Martina tried to calm me down, reminding me it was possible Natalie wasn't even missing. Rationally, I understood that we had no proof yet. But we both knew we needed to check in on Caleb Mercer either way. Eli was staying behind at the office in case Natalie came back, and to keep pressing the building management for security footage. That footage would tell us if she walked out on her own or if someone dragged her away.

Still, everything inside me screamed that she was in danger. I could feel it in my bones. The snow globe alone, the creepy object smeared with blood, was enough to tell me to be worried. My phone buzzed, vibrating against the console. I answered via bluetooth. "Hey Tatum, it's Maddox. You're on speaker."

"Any word from Natalie?"

"No. We're on our way to check out Caleb Mercer's apartment in Oakland. He might be involved."

"The team just started running background on him. So far he's clean. Do you think he's our killer?"

"He could be our guy, or not. But it's a name, and our best lead at this point."

"Let us know if you need backup."

"Will do. Any updates from the lab or the research team?

"We just got the DNA back on the blood from the snow globe. It's a match to James Stamford, one of the victims from the third crime scene."

I let out a slow breath. "So we now know it was the killer who dropped it off on Natalie's porch."

"Or gave it to someone else to drop off. Either way, it's definitely connected to the scene."

"Any prints?"

"No prints. No fibers. But CSU says it looked like the dinner was cooked shortly before the victims died. The M.E. estimates their time of death between ten and twelve last night, about twenty-four hours ago. But here's the weird part. There was no sign on either victim that they had been cooking. No food splatters or traces of food on their hands or under their fingernails. And the kitchen was free of fingerprints, splatters, and there were no dishes in the sink."

I frowned. "Could they have cleaned up after and then showered and changed their clothes?"

"Not likely. It's more likely our suspect killed them and then made a feast in their home."

The thought turned my stomach. "That is... weird."

"Gray and Rodriguez have been questioning the family and friends. Nobody had plans to come over to have dinner with the Stamfords. So yeah, we think the killer went in, and either killed them before he started cooking or after."

"What about other fibers? Anything on the Santa suit from the first crime scene? That one was unique."

"We tracked the suit online. Subpoenas are in for the company's customer logs, but nothing back yet."

"What about ballistics?"

"Should be coming in soon. Dr. Lang already extracted the bullets from the victims. The lab's working overnight. Nobody wants a serial killer running around the Bay Area at Christmas, or at any time, for that matter."

"Call me if you find anything else."

"Will do. And, if you need back up, don't hesitate to call."

With a sigh, I said, "Okay," and ended the call.

I glanced at Martina. "Why would he take her?" All I could think about was Natalie. The forensics were practically of no use to us in this situation.

"I think he wants her to tell his story. And if he took her, he's taking her somewhere to write the article."

"And then what will he do with her?"

Martina shrugged. "Anybody's guess. He may not want to hurt her, but feel he has no choice. It's important we find her, and fast."

Obviously.

Distracted by the conversation, I slammed on my brakes as a red flashed in front of us. My chest lurched against the seat belt, and I blew out a sharp breath. "Sorry."

"Do you want me to drive?"

"We're almost there."

Moments later, I spotted the Oakland apartment building and slid into a parking spot directly in front, a small miracle at this hour. *Thank you, Karma.*

We headed for the lobby doors and found they were locked, access only granted with a key. Martina tilted her head. "Why don't you look away for a minute?"

"What do you mean?"

"Look away. Maybe the door's unlocked." She winked.

Martina never struck me as the shady type, but she was a private investigator. She said she'd do whatever it took to get Natalie back. Maybe her means weren't exactly legal, but right now I didn't care, I just wanted Natalie safe. So if she told me to look away, I was going to look away. I heard a faint click and forced myself not to glance over my shoulder.

"Look," Martina called a moment later. "The door's open."

I turned, shooting her a glance. "There *are* security cameras."

"It's fine." She smirked, already pushing inside.

We spotted the stairwell and jogged toward it. The apartment was on the third floor. I pushed open the door and took the steps two at a time. Martina hurried behind me. She was ten years older than me, but she was in darn good shape. I was glad she could keep up.

At the third floor, I yanked the door open and held it for her. My weapon was at my side, my pulse pounding in my ears as we moved down the hallway.

Apartment 327.

I raised my fist and knocked.

We were met with silence. Martina stepped up and knocked again. We stood still, listening for any signs of life inside.

"I don't think there's anybody inside," I whispered.

"I don't think so either," Martina said. Then her eyes flicked to mine. "But I'd like to know for sure. Why don't you take a walk?"

I smiled faintly. "I'll just look away."

Maybe there was a part of me that could get used to this PI life, working on the fringes of the law to do what had to be done. "Look at that," Martina said a beat later, pushing the door open. "It's unlocked."

Playing along, I said, "Did you hear that?"

Martina tipped her head. "I think someone is calling for help? It's muffled."

I didn't usually operate outside the law, but these weren't usual circumstances. Weapons raised, we stepped inside. The place was small. A Christmas tree stood in the corner, decorated in red, yellow, green, and blue, with a gold star perched on top. Family photos lined the wall, just like at the Mercer home in Orinda. We swept the apartment quickly. It didn't take long. It wasn't a big place. "She's not here," Martina said flatly as we met back in the living room.

"We need to drive to San Francisco."

With a nod, we stepped out of the apartment and readied ourselves for what came next. As we reached the outside, I thought, *Where are you, Natalie?* I checked my phone again, praying for a text from her. There were none.

37

HIM

Natalie was an interesting person. She seemed calm, faster on the keys than I expected as she typed away on her laptop. Of course, she was frustrated that I had disconnected the Wi-Fi and blocked any chance of a hotspot. Her phone was sealed in a Faraday bag. Nobody would trace her through cell signals or GPS. Not until I was finished with her.

She was beautiful in her own way. Not dolled up like some women her age. She was authentic. Part of me wanted to get to know her better. And why not? We had all night.

It felt good to talk. To tell my story out loud. Nobody else wanted to hear it, but people needed to know. Yes, my crimes may appear gruesome, and maybe they wouldn't understand at first, but Natalie would help me make them understand. I wasn't some sadistic killer who got a thrill from frightening people. I had a purpose. A drive. A mission. It was important work.

I wasn't like those other killers. Not like Ted Bundy, who preyed on women, using them for his own sick desires before murdering them. *Disgusting.* Or John Wayne Gayce and so many others. Monsters who lived double lives—family, church, kids—while secretly torturing and killing the innocent. BTK, Dennis

Rader, comes to mind. He had it all, and still bound, tortured, and killed. Even a child. Innocents.

I didn't kill innocents. Not unless I absolutely had to. And I never had to.

Natalie would be fine, as long as she kept up her end of the bargain. If she didn't fight me, didn't try to contact anyone afterward, didn't scream or try to escape, then she would live. But I could see the fight in her eyes. If she pushed me, our arrangement might end in blood. And cleanup. Cleanup was such a pain. It wasn't a part that I enjoyed.

But the aftermath, that was something else. After eliminating one of the wretched parasites who had hurt so many others, I felt... clear. Calm. Like finishing a meditation.

The Stamfords had been no different. I wanted them to have that Christmas dinner. It was part of the scene I was setting, and in a way it was cathartic. I'd always enjoyed cooking. Never had many people to cook for, though. My family, sometimes, though they were overbearing. Always hovering, always demanding. College. Law school. Corporate law, like Daddy. And yes, I did it. But I hated it. The paycheck was good, sure. The flexible hours gave me time—time to plan something meaningful.

Unlike other killers, I wasn't destroying lives for sport. The result of my work was simple. My work improved the world for others.

"How's it coming along, Natalie?"

She didn't look up. "It's good. I usually do a few rounds of editing, so this might take a while. I want to get it just right."

At first she'd been terrified, but now she looked almost invigorated. Maybe this was what she always looked like when she wrote a story. Did she realize the honor I'd given her? A firsthand account of what would become a notorious serial killer? Of course, she couldn't call me Dexter. They'd laugh her out of the newsroom. She didn't know my name, my life, my location, and neither did the police. That was the benefit of being smarter than nearly everyone else.

Detective Kate Maddox was not a challenge to outsmart, neither was Martina Monroe. Don't get me wrong, I had the utmost respect for Martina Monroe, she was sharp and unrelenting. But she didn't have my intelligence, my foresight, nor my planning. Once Natalie's article came out, they would see. They'd know where to look. They'd understand. They'd have no choice but to act. To change the system. To save the children.

"Can I get you anything, Natalie?"

"I'd love some water."

"Are you hungry? I have some snacks, not the healthiest though."

"Sure. What've you got?"

She wasn't afraid of me, not really. Not on the surface. That would work in my favor. I returned with cookies, a bag of chips, and a plastic bottle of water. All that packaging was wasteful, yes, but leaving no trace mattered more. "Here you go. Let's have a break."

"Okay." She popped open the bag of chips and twisted the cap off the water. Took a sip, then a bite. "So... why me?" she asked.

I smiled. "I read your other articles. Especially 'Blood on the Mistletoe.' Very insightful. The holidays are stressful, Natalie. Most people don't realize that."

"Thanks. So after this, when I'm done, you'll let me go?"

"Don't worry about that. As long as you keep your end of the bargain, you're safe."

She hesitated, chewing on her lip. I could practically see the questions swirling in her mind. "You can ask me anything, Natalie. I'll tell you what I can."

"What if... what if someone like Kate or Martina found us? What would you do then?"

I grinned, amused. "They won't."

"But if they did—"

"They won't," I repeated, sharper that time. "Kate Maddox is emotional. She lets her feelings cloud her judgment. She's too reckless to catch me. And Martina Monroe, she's clever, I'll give her that. I respect her. But clever isn't enough. Not against me. I've planned for everything."

Natalie's throat bobbed as she swallowed.

"As long as you keep your end of the bargain," I went on smoothly, "you're safe. No one is coming, Natalie. Not tonight. Not until I'm finished with you."

She looked away, silent, and I let the moment stretch before steering the conversation back. "I've been thinking about a question you asked earlier," I said. "Why I killed the way I did. We'll get to that. But first, tell me more about you. What drives you as a crime reporter? You're good at it. You've got a close friend at the police department. Why do you do it?"

"Well, I guess I want people to know the dangers out there. To take precautions. Not that it should be on individuals to avoid being killed or hurt, but it's good to be cautious. Also I'd like people to understand the impact of crime. If someone's thinking of committing one, like a burglary, they should know what it does to the victims. The way it shatters a home, a sense of safety. Maybe they'd think twice. Maybe they wouldn't. Maybe I'm just a dreamer."

I studied her. She was fascinating. "That's interesting, Natalie. You listen to a lot of true crime, don't you?"

"I do. Podcasts. Documentaries. Books. Memoirs."

"Perhaps you and I are more alike than you think. I do the same."

She tilted her head. "Really?"

"Yes. That's how I built my plan. Reading about other killers.

And you know what I realized? Most of them are just trash human beings. I'm not. I have purpose. And so do you."

She raised her brows.

"I mean it. I think life will bring you great things, Natalie. And when the police figure this out, when they finally put the pieces together, it'll be because of your article. I want you to work with Martina Monroe. I've followed her for years. She's exposed plenty of atrocities. She can help you push this further."

Natalie nodded slowly.

"Good." I leaned back, satisfied. "So—what do you do for fun?"

She gave a half-smile. "Fun? Honestly, I watch TV, documentaries, podcasts... go to the gym. Hang out with Kate."

"All work and no play," I teased.

"My work can be consuming."

"I can understand that."

She glanced at me, curiosity sparking. "What do you do for work?"

I chuckled. "Oh, that's boring. Trust me. What we're doing here, this is much more important. Much more interesting. You'll see."

38

MARTINA

The lights on the Bay Bridge glittered as we crossed into downtown San Francisco. It was a clear and beautiful night, if you ignored the fact that a killer was running loose. My phone vibrated. I snatched it up. "Selena, what did you find?"

"I'm here with Vincent too," she said.

"Hey, Vincent."

"Hey, Martina," he said. "We have a description. She was definitely taken."

My gut tightened. "What happened?"

"You can tell from a traffic cam across the street," Selena explained. "She met someone, shook hands. Then, quick as a flash, he injected something into her neck. She slumped, and he carried her out the front door. Absolutely no question, she was abducted."

A cold rush went through me. "Did you see what car he put her in?"

"We sure did," Vincent said.

I glanced at Kate, my pulse hammering.

"The car is registered to Caleb Mercer," Selena continued.

"We've got the Oakland and San Francisco addresses already flagged. Have you checked them out yet?"

"We went to Oakland. The apartment was empty," I said. "We're on our way to San Francisco now."

"Do you want us to meet you for backup?" Vincent asked.

"Might be a good idea."

"What about OPD?"

I shook my head even though they couldn't see me. "We don't exactly have probable cause. Not with how we acquired the ID."

"True, true," Vincent said. "All right. We'll meet you at the San Francisco address."

"Thanks, Vincent. Thanks, Selena." I ended the call.

Kate's eyes flicked toward me.

With a nod, I said, "It's him. Caleb Mercer. He took her."

"What do you mean? How do you know?"

I explained what Selena and Vincent had found on the traffic cam footage, the injection, and the abduction.

Kate side-eyed me. "I see how you get the job done."

"Emphasis on *get the job done*."

"You're not getting an argument from me," she said. "They're going to meet us there?"

"They're about thirty minutes out. If this goes sideways, we'll have Vincent and Selena as backup. And we can call in more if we need to."

"I should call it in," Kate said. "At least let them know where we're going."

"Yes. But we don't have legal probable cause to storm in guns blazing."

"True, but if we hear her in there, I'm going in."

I prayed for Natalie, and prayed we were heading to the right place. But the thought gnawed at me, what if he'd taken her somewhere else? A hotel, or an abandoned property?

I quickly called Selena back. "Did you find anything in his financials to determine if he checked into a hotel or rented a car?"

Kate raised a brow at me.

Selena didn't hesitate. "Not yet. Do you want me to do it and wait to meet you, or should I hand it off?"

"Have someone else from the office handle it. You come with Vincent. We'll need backup in San Francisco."

"You got it."

I ended the call.

Kate shook her head, a small smile forming on her lips. "People just jump when you ask, don't they?"

"Usually," I said. "But they also know I'd take a bullet for them."

"Understood. Now I know who to call if I ever need help."

"Absolutely. Anytime. And if you ever want to switch careers…"

"You've definitely given me a few things to think about. Let's get Natalie and this guy first. Then maybe we'll talk."

We pulled up in front of Caleb Mercer's apartment building in San Francisco. There was no parking in sight. Kate cursed under her breath, then double-parked. We jumped out of the vehicle and rushed toward the entrance. On the way, I said a silent prayer, *Please let Natalie be unharmed.*

39

MARTINA

The front door of the apartment building was locked. I paused, thumb hovering over my lock-pick set, and used the moment to fire off a quick text to Selena.

> We've arrived at Mercer's place. Going in.

"Are you going to let your team know we're moving in?" I asked Kate, eyes flicking over the street behind us.

"Yeah," she whispered. "I just did."

Before I could kneel down to work the lock, luck was on our side. A resident pushed through from inside. Kate flashed her badge. The man barely looked at us, earbuds in, before disappearing into the night. We slipped inside and headed for the stairwell. My pulse thudded louder with every flight. By the time we reached the sixth floor, my mouth was dry, and my palms were slick.

Mercer's door, 613, sat at the end of a corridor. I scanned the corners. No cameras. Just us. I turned to Kate. "I'll knock first. If no one answers, we're going in."

She nodded, knowing what it meant. Protocol be damned, Natalie's life outweighed rules. We moved in tandem, weapons drawn, closing in on the door. I rapped my knuckles against it and stepped back. We listened, but were met with silence.

I knocked again, then pressed my ear to the door. My heartbeat hammered so loud I almost missed it, the faint scuff of movement inside. I froze and then lifted a finger to signal Kate to wait.

Silence again.

We retreated a few steps down the hallway. "How do you want to play this?" I said quietly. "I think someone's in there. If I use the lock-pick, he might hear it and panic. We should go in fast and surprise him."

Kate arched a skeptical brow. "Do you have a lot of experience kicking down doors?"

"I've kicked down a few," I deadpanned. "It's not as hard as it looks."

She smirked, but she gave the smallest nod. *Decision made.*

I crept back to the door, with adrenaline humming through my veins. I braced myself. One hard kick, and a boom sounded as the doorframe's wood splintered and the door slammed open, crashing against the wall.

Inside, the scene stopped me in my tracks.

Natalie, eyes wide, was pinned in the man's grip, his arm locked around her throat. A gun pressed against her temple.

"Police!" Kate shouted, with her weapon trained on the man. "Put the gun down. Now!"

The man, Caleb Mercer, if we were right, smiled, but it didn't reach his eyes. "I don't think so," he said, and tightened his grip on Natalie.

Kate remained calm. "What do you want?"

"I want you to leave. Leave and she'll be fine. Right, Natalie?"

Natalie's eyes widened as she tried to nod.

He continued, "Natalie knows I have no desire to hurt her or you, Detective Maddox, but I also have no desire to go to prison." He paused and eyed me. "You must be Martina Monroe. So lovely to make your acquaintance. I only wish it were under better circumstances."

Was it possible we could negotiate? "I've been wanting to talk to you too, Caleb."

He nodded, yet his weapon and grip on Natalie was unwavering. "I should have known you would figure it out, Miss Monroe. If anyone could, it would be you."

If he knew I'd figure it out, why send me the Christmas cards? "Isn't that what you wanted?"

He looked me in the eyes. "I wanted you to know what they did. What they continue to do. I believe whole-heartedly you are the one who could bring them to justice. Although, I am a bit surprised your sidekick, retired sergeant Hirsch, isn't here with you."

Kate said, "Nope. She's stuck with me."

Kate was agitated, but I needed to keep the situation calm if we were going to get Natalie, and ourselves, out of there alive.

He cocked his head. "Not a bad choice for a new partner, I suppose. Our mutual friend, Natalie here, has told me she is quite fond of Detective Maddox. You do seem to have a spark."

Kate inched closer. "Cut the crap. What do you want in exchange for Natalie's safety?"

Shaking his head, "No patience. Didn't your parents ever tell you that patience is what Santa brings on Christmas?"

"No."

"That's right. Your parents died when you were little and you had the unfortunate experience of the foster system. I am truly sorry for that. And I am quite impressed you've done so well in life. Well, done. Not all of them were that lucky."

"How would you know? You didn't grow up in the system."

"I knew someone who did. Someone I cared deeply for. Unfortunately, the scar had run too deep."

"I'm sorry to hear that."

As Kate continued the conversation with Caleb, I considered whether I had a clean shot. Would he see the squeeze of the trigger? Would he know I would take him out without hesitation?

He continued, "Yes, it was quite heart-breaking to see her spiral out of control like that. She died, you know. On Christmas Eve. Christmas could never be the same after that."

That answered the question regarding the timing of the kills.

"Was she a victim of the 2005 Christmas fire in Oakland?" Kate asked.

"No, that was well before I knew her. But I see you've been doing your homework."

That meant we had gone down the wrong track with Robert Flurry, the survivor of the fire. Perhaps that was Caleb's intention all along. The other question burning in my mind was, was he distracted enough? Or could we distract him enough to take him out?

Before I could prepare for the shot, I heard footsteps nearing the apartment. With a quick glance I saw it was civilians, likely Caleb's neighbors. I shouted, "Police! Move away from the apartment."

The neighbors hurried away. The police would show up soon, that was either a good thing or a bad thing. Time was running out.

Caleb narrowed his eyes. "I think it's time for the two of you to leave."

With a sincere gaze, and even tone, I said, "Caleb. It's over. We understand what you were trying to do. Natalie will tell your story. And I will work with Kate to get justice for the foster kids who need our help. But you need to let Natalie go. We can end this peacefully."

He shook his head, and his eyes went dark. "Unfortunately, I don't think we can."

40

NATALIE

My heart nearly beat out of my chest as his arm locked tighter around my throat, the gun now fixed on Martina and Kate. I had never been more terrified in my life. I knew what he was capable of. I'd studied his patterns, understood his motives. That knowledge offered no comfort, because if I, or they, pushed him the wrong way, we'd all die in this apartment. And in his own words, he said this wouldn't end peacefully. Of course not. I knew that from talking with him this evening. What could I do?

The bang of the door being kicked in still echoed in my ears. Surely the neighbors heard it. Surely the police were already on their way. Backup had to be coming. *Please, God, let backup be coming.*

Sweat slid down my face, stinging my eyes. My chest burned with shallow, frantic breaths. I risked a glance at him, Dexter, or Caleb, or whatever his real name was. My voice came out hoarse, trembling. "If you kill me, the article won't go out."

His only response was to tighten his grip, cutting off another gasp of air. "Not true, Natalie. It's on your computer. I can email it to your editor myself. Or to the New York Times or to everyone. My story doesn't end with you."

He was right, but it was worth a shot. Assessing the situation, it was two against one. Three if you counted me. What could I do?

Could Martina and Kate shoot him before he pulled the trigger? I wanted to believe they could. I had to. Tears spilled down my cheeks, hot and humiliating, as flashes of my life surged through me, my parents' faces, gone too soon. College. The thrill of my first byline. The reckless decision to meet a source when I knew a killer was out there, a killer who knew me by name, and where I lived. What had I really done in my twenty-nine years? Would anyone remember me if I died here tonight?

I sniffed hard, lifting my gaze. Kate's eyes locked on mine, fierce and unyielding. Determination blazed there, and I had no doubt she'd rather die than let him win. Martina, too. Both women radiated a steely resolve I'd never seen before. And that's when it hit me.

Maybe I wasn't powerless.

Maybe I could help.

I gave the slightest nod, a tiny signal Kate couldn't miss, then squeezed my eyes shut. I only had one chance, and I had to take it.

41

DETECTIVE KATE MADDOX

From this angle I had a clear shot—clear, except for Natalie's trembling body now locked against his chest. One wrong move, one twitch of his trigger finger, and she was gone. My hands ached from the pressure of holding my weapon steady, my finger on the trigger, my breath caught somewhere high in my throat.

Then I saw it, the smallest nod from Natalie, a signal to me. She was going to do something or she was preparing to make peace with a terrible fate. *Not on my watch.*

As she squeezed her eyes shut, she moved. Her heel slammed down on his foot, hard enough to make him grunt. He faltered, just for a heartbeat, his focus slipping.

My chest seized.

It was now or never.

I aimed at center mass and squeezed the trigger. The blast split the air, deafening. A moment later another shot rang out. His body jerked violently, the gun wrenched sideways as his knees buckled. He dragged Natalie half a step with him before crashing to the floor, blood spreading beneath him. His leg was bloodied and bent unnaturally. The second shot had been from Martina.

Natalie stumbled forward into my arms. She was sobbing, shaking, but alive. As I held her tight, Martina ran over and kicked away his weapon and checked on his injuries. Had it been a kill shot? I sure as heck hoped so.

42

MARTINA

Turned on his back, blood pooled beneath Caleb, and was spreading. Kate's shot hit him in the chest, but it may not be fatal. His knee, shredded from my shot, left him writhing and groaning in agony. He wasn't dead yet. He might even have a chance at surviving, which meant spending the rest of his life behind bars.

If Natalie hadn't acted, if she hadn't been brave enough to fight back, we might not have had this opening at all. She'd been smart, and braver than most. I'd already kicked his weapon across the room, but I didn't trust him not to rally. Monsters like him had a way of finding strength even when they shouldn't have any left. I kept my gun trained on him. "You got cuffs?" I asked.

Kate's voice came behind me. "Do you need them?"

"I do."

My eyes stayed locked on Caleb as Kate passed them forward. His eyes were open, glassy but still searching, staring at me like he couldn't quite believe what had happened. I grabbed his arms and cuffed his wrists. The silver bracelets were a Christmas present to the Bay Area.

Staring down at him, I pressed my palms against his chest, trying to slow the bleeding, his face twisted in pain. I wasn't God. I didn't get to decide who lived or died. I could only make sure the innocent stayed safe. That was the difference between us, he'd chosen vengeance. I chose justice.

Behind me, I heard Kate. "I'll call it in."

Sirens already wailed faintly in the distance, someone else in the building must have dialed it in when we broke down the door. Still, it mattered that Kate got the word out. The Christmas Killer was caught. He would never hurt anyone again. Although, from what we had learned about his victims, I wouldn't shed a tear for any of them. That still didn't make what he did justified.

Caleb bucked with his good leg, trying to twist away from my grip. His voice came raw and broken. "Tell them, Martina. You have to tell them."

"I will," I said, as my heart pounded. "We'll get them."

For the first time in my career, after decades of taking down mobsters, corrupt cops, and organized crime syndicates, I felt like I'd overlooked something. The foster system. The kids who slipped through the cracks. The ones no one had protected.

I looked at Caleb's face. His grimace, his pain. And beneath it, a hollow grief. "What was her name?" I asked quietly.

His lips trembled. A ragged breath escaped. "Linnea. She was... so beautiful."

The name hit me like a kick to the chest. Linnea Porter. I'd seen it in the case files, the CPS reports. She'd lived in both the Slade and the Stamford homes. She'd overdosed last Christmas. Another lost girl no one had saved, but it sounds like maybe Caleb had tried.

I tightened my hands on his chest, feeling his heartbeat falter under my palms. "We'll get justice for her, Caleb. For Linnea."

His gaze softened. A bloody smile tugged at his mouth, then

faded as his eyes began to close. Blood seeped fast between my fingers as I pressed down. Caleb's chest hitched under my hands, every breath a ragged rattle.

His eyes opened slightly and stayed fixed on me, wild one moment, hollow the next, like he couldn't decide if I was his executioner or his confessor. I'd seen that look before. His lips moved as blood bubbled at the corners. "Linnea," he rasped again, as if the name itself might keep him there. His face twisted, half a grimace, half a plea.

I leaned closer, forcing my voice steady. "We'll get justice for Linnea." And for an instant, I saw him not as a killer, but as a sad, heartbroken man. Then the fight bled out of him. His body sagged, his chest stilled beneath my hands. The light drained from his eyes, leaving nothing but a glassy stare at the ceiling.

I sat back on my heels. Kate was still on the phone, her voice urgent, reporting it in. Natalie clung to her side, sobbing into her shoulder.

For a long beat I just knelt there, hands slick with blood, staring at the lifeless man who had brought Christmas terror to the city. The sirens sounded closer now, echoing through the streets below. They'd find him cuffed, secured, but already gone.

It was over.

But even as I rose to my feet, my knees stiff, my heart heavy, one thought burned sharper than the rest. *Linnea Porter*. A name that had lived only in forgotten files, in the silence of a grave, and now dragged into the light by a man who had twisted grief into violence. She deserved better. They all did.

43

NATALIE

My body wouldn't stop shaking. Every nerve buzzed, like electricity humming just under my skin. Kate holding my hand was the only thing keeping me upright, the only thing stopping me from slipping to the floor.

I wanted to close my eyes, to shut it all out, but I couldn't. My gaze locked on Caleb where he sprawled on the carpet, blood soaked through his shirt.

He was dead. It wasn't what I wanted. From what he'd told me, he wasn't all bad. But he was bad enough to go to prison for the rest of his life. I hated myself for it, but part of me wanted to hear what he'd say next. He'd told me his story, but was it the whole story? Did he have more to tell? He had done awful things, but he was still a person. A person who had felt deeply and been hurt terribly.

I knew what he'd been fighting for, twisted as it was. I'd read between the lines of his story, and hearing him say her name, Linnea, sent a chill down my spine that no amount of Kate's warmth could chase away. If we had all died here tonight, no one would have ever told her story.

Tears streamed hot down my cheeks, blurring my vision. My

throat ached where his arm had pressed tight, and every breath came shallow, but I forced myself to look. Forced myself to remember. Kate's voice broke through. "Don't look at him. He can't hurt you anymore."

But she didn't understand. He already had. And unless I wrote it, unless I finished what I'd started, that hurt would never heal.

44

MARTINA

Minutes later, the hallway exploded into chaos. Boots thundered down the hall as the SWAT team flooded in, shouted commands, radios squawking, and hands gripping weapons even though the fight was already over.

"Suspect down!" Kate barked. "One hostage recovered, and she needs immediate medical."

Paramedics shouldered past the first wave of law enforcement. They dropped beside Caleb, their gloves snapping as they muscled me out of the way. My body sagged with the sudden movement, as if the fight drained out of me in the same moment.

"Vitals?" one medic demanded.

Another shook his head, already sliding paddles from a case. They went through the motions of trying to save him, but even from a few feet away I could see it was too late. Caleb was gone, or close enough that no amount of tubes and jolts would bring him back to life.

I stepped back, weary, letting the crew take over. That was

their role now, not mine. Behind me, Kate was cornered by her team. I caught snippets of conversation, her lieutenant's clipped voice, the half-relieved, half-angry tone of someone who knew she'd gone off script. "You shouldn't have gone in without backup."

Kate's jaw was set, eyes rimmed red, but her chin lifted. "If I hadn't, she'd be dead."

After a long pause, Tatum said, "Well, it looked like a good shot, Maddox, and I'm glad she's okay."

It was clear Kate could fight her own battles and was respected by her direct supervisor. Natalie was another story. Medics wrapped her in a blanket that swallowed her small frame, their voices rapid-fire. "What's your name? Do you know where you are? Any injuries we can't see?" She answered quietly, her lips barely moving.

The indignity of it stung me on her behalf. They treated her like evidence, a fragile piece of property catalogued for the report. And maybe that was necessary, but I saw what they didn't. The way her eyes flicked back, over and over, to Caleb's body on the floor. Likely the grip around her neck was still there, etched into her memory, even if he had already expired.

I wanted to go across the room, to sit beside her, to tell her she'd done more than survive, she'd been the one who shifted the fight. But words felt useless in this flood of noise. I found myself in the hallway waiting for the police and paramedics to do their thing before I could reconnect with Kate and Natalie.

My phone buzzed. A message from Selena.

> We're five minutes out.

I stared at the words a long moment before typing back.

> Suspect down. Police are here. I'll meet you outside in front of the building.

For a moment I thought about Caleb. He hadn't been a monster born out of greed or power. His violence had grown from grief. Was that true? Or had he always been a psychopath that had simply been triggered by Linnea's death? Not all psychopaths became murderers, but Caleb had.

Linnea Porter. A foster kid who'd slipped through every crack until she OD'd last Christmas. I hadn't known her. I hadn't even heard her name aloud until Caleb gasped it out with his dying breath. And yet she'd fueled every decision he'd made since then, every life he'd stolen.

I rubbed at my eyes, suddenly heavy. Too many children like Linnea had been lost, and I hadn't ever thought about it. Surely not all foster homes were bad. Kate was proof of that. It was because of a loving foster mother, the leader of her last group home, that she'd found a career path and had become a successful adult. I really hoped that the Stamfords and the Slades were exceptions, and not the rule.

Before heading downstairs, I wanted to check in with Kate to let her know I was meeting my team. In the hallway, I said, "Nice job in there."

"You too."

"How are you holding up?"

Her shoulders seemed to relax. "I'm just glad Natalie's okay."

"She's lucky to have you."

"I think it's the other way around."

"Maybe it's that you're lucky to have each other."

She nodded.

"My team is downstairs. Do you need me?"

"It should be fine. They can take your statement down there."

"Okay."

After a moment, I stepped forward and embraced her in a hug. We'd been through an ordeal together, and I wanted her to know I understood and that I was there for her.

Upon releasing her, I said, "If you need anything—anything at all—know I'm here."

A small smile formed on her lips. "Thank you, Martina. I do."

With relief, I exited the hallway and made my way out of the chaos.

Outside, the air was chilly, my breath creating a fog. It felt good. The chatter of cops had faded, and for the first time since the door splintered beneath my boot, it was quiet.

From the street, I heard a familiar voice. "Martina?"

I turned to see Selena and Vincent. "Boy am I glad to see the two of you."

And I was. After hugs, I briefed them on the situation. Caleb's reign of Christmas terror was over, but the job wasn't. It was unlikely the OPD would investigate the allegations against the Slades and Stamfords or CPS and any faults in the foster system that needed exposing. But I would, and so would my team. We wouldn't just get justice for Linnea, we'd get it for all who needed it.

A few minutes later we were joined by Kate. After introductions, she said, "Medics are bringing Natalie down. I'm going to ride over to the hospital with her."

"Of course."

The fierce look in her eyes told me she'd carry the memory and trauma of this night forever, but she'd survive it too. She was a survivor and so was Natalie. They had each other, which would carry them through this storm.

After the paramedics came and went and statements had

been taken, Selena, Vinent and I watched as Caleb's body was carted out of the building in a black body bag. Another casualty. The adrenaline that had carried me was gone, leaving me stiff, cold, and coated in someone else's blood. I was ready to go home and be surrounded by the warmth of my family.

45

NATALIE

The ER was too bright and too loud. The fluorescent lights buzzed overhead, the paper sheet beneath me crinkled with every shift, and the smell of antiseptic made my stomach turn. I clutched the blanket they'd draped over me, trying to stop the tremors in my hands. My throat ached where his arm had pinned me, every swallow a reminder.

The door clicked open. Kate slipped inside, her jacket gone and her sleeves rolled up. Damp hair clung to her temples and her eyes were rimmed red, but she was steady and anchored in a way I wasn't. She dragged a chair up beside the bed and sat. "Hey," she said softly. "How are you doing?"

I let out a laugh that wasn't really a laugh. "I don't even know. My body feels like it's humming. And my head..." I pressed a hand against it. "It keeps replaying it. Over and over. Him. The gun."

Kate leaned forward. "That's normal. You're probably still in shock. It'll fade." Her gaze softened. "But you did good in there, Natalie. Better than good. You fought back. You gave me the opening to take the shot."

Tears blurred my vision. I shook my head. "Or I could've

gotten us all killed. I didn't think, I just—" My voice cracked. "I couldn't let him keep control."

Kate tipped her head. "That was survival. You trusted your instincts. And you're alive because of it."

Alive. The word sat heavy in my chest. But his voice echoed there too. *Linnea.*

I swallowed, wincing at the sting in my throat. "When he said her name... Linnea. I felt... I don't know. Sad. He had told me about her, but hadn't said her name until those last moments."

"Martina connected it. Linnea Porter was a foster kid in both homes we were investigating."

I nodded. "He loved her. Obsessively. That grief... it's what drove all of this. He told me about what she went through, and how he tried to help but he couldn't. It really ate at him."

The truth of it pressed down on me. Caleb Mercer was dead, but Linnea had died first, and if I wasn't careful, her story would vanish beneath his. That's what he wanted, that his violence would be remembered as her justice. But it wasn't justice. It never could be.

I wiped at my damp cheeks. "He wanted it to be about him avenging her. Avenging all of them. But if I write it that way, his crimes will eclipse everything. Linnea will only ever be a footnote to his twisted story."

Kate studied me, her brow furrowed. "Then don't write it that way."

The simplicity of her words shook me. "Tell it differently," she said. "Tell it so Linnea is the one remembered, not him. You've already survived him. Don't let him own the story too."

The knot in my chest loosened, just a little. Kate's hand came to rest lightly on my arm. She had a steady and grounding effect about her. Like if I had her in my corner, I could do anything. I clutched the blanket tighter. "That's what I'll do. I'll make sure it's about her. About the kids the system failed. Not him."

Kate gave me the smallest smile, tired but fierce. "Good."

For the first time since the gun barrel pressed into my temple, I believed that not only would I live, but I'd live with a purpose.

46

MARTINA

It had been three days since we caught the Christmas Killer and ensured Natalie's safety, as well as anyone else who had landed on Caleb Mercer's hit list. A search of his apartment in San Francisco confirmed he wasn't finished. He had been plotting his reign of terror for almost a year.

Two more names were on that list. The last victim was meant to die on Christmas Eve. Knowing we had prevented those murders, knowing we had saved at least two more lives, brought me a sense of peace. It also made us curious as to what those intended victims had done to get on his list. We looked into their backgrounds, and theirs were other homes Linnea had been placed in. It was clear from our research they were as bad as the Slades and Stamfords. The police opened an investigation and would prosecute them if they could make a case. I prayed justice would prevail.

The police were also satisfied all three crime scenes were attributed to Caleb Mercer. Ballistics matched the gun found in his San Francisco apartment, and Natalie's story provided not only a motive but also a confession in his own words. If he hadn't died, he would have ended up in prison. One more monster slain.

We never did find Robert Flurry. Perhaps that was a case to solve on another day.

Curled up on the sofa, I cradled a steaming mocha in my hands and watched as the peppermint sprinkles melted into the chocolate. The warmth of the holiday treat seeped into my body as I sipped. In front of me on the coffee table lay a copy of The Bay Insider. Natalie's article filled the front page. I picked it up and began to read. Straight from the start, I knew it wasn't your typical sensationalized serial killer story.

As my eyes moved down the page, I felt the pain in her words, the raw honesty of someone who had seen the darkness and refused to let the victims be reduced to headlines.

∼

BEYOND THE CHRISTMAS KILLER: THE LIFE AND LOSS OF LINNEA PORTER

By Natalie Sloane - The Bay Insider

SAN FRANCISCO, Calif. — The Christmas lights still glowed across the Bay Area when the reign of Christmas terror ended. On Sunday morning, families awoke to headlines announcing the death of the man known as "The Christmas Killer." For the past two weeks, his crimes had cast a shadow over the season. Chimneys, no longer symbols of warmth, and dinner tables remembered for blood instead of joy. Parents kept children indoors. Holiday gatherings carried an undercurrent of fear. Entire neighborhoods watched the calendar with dread.

It ended in a San Francisco apartment, where police fatally shot Caleb Mercer after a hostage standoff. His death brought relief, but also questions: Who was this man? Why Christmas? And why now? For the first time, we have answers.

A Motive Born of Grief

In a misguided attempt to tell his story, Mercer took me hostage. He wanted the world to know his mission, convinced his killings were not crimes but a twisted form of justice. At the center of it all was his late girlfriend, Linnea Porter.

Linnea grew up in foster care, shuffled from home to home, her life marked by trauma and neglect. Mercer told me she turned to drugs to escape those memories. Despite his efforts to help her get clean, Linnea overdosed and died on Christmas Eve last year. Her death became his obsession, a wound that never healed, a loss he tried to avenge through bloodshed.

A Trail of Violence.

Mercer's killings unfolded like a macabre advent calendar, each crime tied to the holiday. His victims included Garrett Slade, a man discovered wedged inside a chimney. Margaret Lawson, a woman killed in a bathtub and decorated with Christmas lights. Lastly, James and Julie Stamford, a couple, shot and posed at their dining table as if still awaiting Christmas dinner.

They were all connected by one chilling thread: Linnea's past as a foster child; the Slades and Stamfords her foster parents and Lawson the CPS case manager assigned to her. Investigators now believe Mercer chose his victims deliberately, attempting to punish those he believed had failed her. His staging was grotesque but calculated, a demand that the city, and perhaps the world, look at her suffering.

The terror ended on the sixth floor of a San Francisco apartment. Mercer held me at gunpoint, his voice breaking as he begged me to write Linnea's story. When police stormed the room, he was shot. His final word was her name.

To recount his crimes in lurid detail would grant Mercer the notoriety he craved. But to ignore them would erase the lives he stole. His violence scarred this city. Yet his story should never eclipse Linnea's.

A System in Crisis.

Linnea's life was not an anomaly—it was a reflection of a system that fails too many. Today, more than 437,000 children live in foster care across the United States. Their odds are grim. Only about half graduate high school on time. In California, it's just 53%, compared to 83% statewide. By age 21, 23% experience homelessness, 26% have been incarcerated, and nearly half struggle with unemployment well into their mid-20s. Fewer than 8% will ever earn a college degree. These are not just numbers. They are futures lost before they began.

Stories of Change.

Yet there are signs of progress. Across the country, programs are proving that when compassion and resources align, outcomes improve. California's Dec My Dorm initiative provides foster youth entering college with bedding, lamps, and essentials—small things that carry dignity at a critical life stage. And Texas' College Bound Docket transforms courtrooms into supportive spaces where teens plan education, housing, and employment. Since 2019, it has helped more than a hundred youth and provided tuition waivers until age 27. And Missouri's family preservation pilot shifts funding into early interventions, keeping more children safely in their homes. These efforts don't erase the failures, but they point to what is possible.

Remembering Linnea.

Linnea Porter's life followed a trajectory that was tragically common: multiple placements, fractured communities, and a system that gave her few chances to thrive. She was not a symbol of vengeance, nor a justification for violence. She was a young woman who deserved better. If her name forces us to confront uncomfortable truths—graduation gaps, homelessness, and the struggles of aging out unprepared—then her life carries meaning beyond the shadow of Mercer's crimes. Linnea Porter. May we never forget her—not as the obsession of a killer, but as a young woman who should have had a future.

Wiping the tear from the corner of my eye, I was proud of Natalie. I had only known her for a short time, but it was clear she truly cared about people. She wasn't a sensationalist chasing the gory details of terrible crimes. Yes, she reported on them, but always with a sense of humanity and responsibility—an undercurrent of hope that people might love one another a little more, and care for one another a little deeper. I believed she carried that compassion in her bones.

Finished with the article, I set my phone down. Charlie sat beside me on the couch, Barney bounding happily up next to him.

"Did you finish reading the article?" he asked.

"I did. It's pretty spectacular."

"That was my thought as well. She's very talented."

"Yeah."

Charlie leaned back. "You know, her ordeal would make a great true crime book."

As a writer, he had that instinct. "Perhaps you should talk to her about that today."

Both Natalie and Kate had no close blood relatives, yet the two of them had forged a bond like sisters. Kate watching over Natalie, and Natalie looking up to Kate with trust and admiration. It was special, a reminder that family wasn't always about blood. Sometimes people like them needed more than protection. They needed belonging.

As if on cue, the doorbell rang and Barney barked his excited announcement that our first Christmas guests had arrived. I rose to my feet, meeting Zoey and Henry in the hallway as she stepped toward the door.

I said, "I'll get it." If it were Natalie or Kate, I didn't want them to be met by a stranger. With a quick glance at Zoey, I couldn't help but think about how it was so wonderful to have her home. There was no place I wanted her more than here, in our home, with Henry at her side. He doted on her the way he should, and I couldn't imagine Christmas without them both.

Peeking through the window, I spotted Natalie and Kate on the porch. They must have decided to carpool. I pulled open the door. "Merry Christmas!"

"Merry Christmas," they echoed back, smiling.

"Come on in."

Charlie appeared at my shoulder, reaching for their coats. "Let me grab those," he said, hanging them neatly in the hall closet.

"Natalie, Kate, this man stealing your coats is my husband, Charlie," I said, gesturing toward him. Behind me, Zoey snickered with Selena. "And of course you've already met Selena. This is my daughter Zoey and her husband, Henry." *Her husband.* Would I ever get used to that? "And down at your feet is Barney. He likes to greet absolutely everyone who comes through this door."

"Hello, Barney," Natalie said kneeling down to give him a few affectionate scratches. Barney leaned into it, tail wagging with approval.

"Why don't you come on in," I said. "Charlie's made an assortment of beverages. Hot cocoa, coffee, whatever you like."

"Hot cocoa sounds great," Natalie said, her face lighting up as she stepped inside.

"I'd love a coffee," Kate said.

Charlie smiled. "We've got whipped cream, peppermint sprinkles, and I can make it a mocha."

Kate's eyes lit up. "That sounds amazing."

"It is," I told her with a grin. "I'm on my second one of the day."

I led them into the living room where Barney was already tossing a toy across the floor, seeing if anyone wanted to join him in trying to defeat the stuffed gingerbread man.

"Very festive," Kate said, glancing at the decorated tree, the stockings along the mantel, and the faint scent of cinnamon candles in the air.

"I don't usually do a whole lot, but this year the family insisted."

Selena leaned closer and murmured under her breath, "And there aren't any dead bodies, so it's pretty good."

Kate smirked.

As I expected, the two had become fast friends.

Charlie returned with hot cocoas and coffees, steam curling up from the mugs. Selena sat cross-legged on the rug, giggling as Barney pressed his head into her lap. Zoey perched on the couch with Henry, their hands clasped together.

"Please, make yourselves at home."

Sitting on the sofa, Natalie said, "So who else is coming?"

"Hirsch and his family will be over pretty soon," I said, ticking names off on my fingers. "Vincent, and his family, my mom and her husband, Ted. My brother and his family. It's going to be a full house."

"It's so nice to have a big family," Natalie said softly.

"Most of them we found along the journey of life," I said with a smile.

Kate nodded. "That's right. You work with Vincent, and you worked with Hirsch."

"Yep. One big happy family at Drakos Monroe." I chuckled. "Well... most of the time. And we're always looking for great talent," I teased. "If you ever want to give up the badge..."

Kate laughed. "I don't know if I'm quite ready for that. But you nearly changed my mind, seeing what you're able to do in such a short amount of time. It's pretty incredible."

"We have a great team."

"I see that."

I settled onto the sofa beside them. "Your article was amazing, Natalie."

"Oh, thank you." Her cheeks flushed.

Charlie leaned forward. "Very impressive."

He and I exchanged a look. I said, "Charlie's a writer too. He's published three books now."

Natalie's eyes widened. "Really?"

"Yep," Charlie said with a grin. "Greatest job in the world." He hesitated, then asked, "Have you ever considered writing a book? Maybe about your experience?"

She nodded, her face lighting up. "Do you think it'd be a good idea?"

"Absolutely. If you want any pointers getting your first manuscript done, I'd be happy to help."

"Wow. I might take you up on that. Thank you so much."

As the small talk carried on, I looked around my living room, filled with laughter and warmth, and felt a swell of joy. Perhaps I had never known so much of it.

The doorbell rang again. Barney barked loudly and scrambled after Selena, who went to answer it.

"Around here, Barney's head of security," Charlie joked.

The room laughed.

Moments later, Selena returned with Audrey, who squealed in delight as she chased Barney around the living room. She grabbed one of his toys, a stuffed candy cane, and the two wrestled for it before she tossed it across the room. Barney bounded after it, triumphant.

I rose from the couch, arms open. "Merry Christmas, Kim! Hirsch! And merry Christmas, Audrey."

"Merry Christmas to you too," Kim said warmly.

Hirsch gave me a side squeeze, "Merry Christmas."

Audrey giggled. "Merry Christmas, everyone!"

Zoey bent toward her. "Possibly another future veterinarian," she teased. Zoey had babysat Audrey when she was younger, and I thought maybe some of that love for animals had rubbed off.

"Let me do introductions," I said, guiding Kim and Audrey toward Kate and Natalie. Soon everyone was mingling like old friends, laughter and conversation weaving together.

I couldn't help but think how lucky we all were to have found each other. Maybe it was timing, or simply the luck of where we worked, but I liked to believe it was bigger than that. That somehow God or the universe had connected us. That we were meant to find one another.

Family wasn't always blood. Sometimes it was the people who showed up, who stood by you in darkness, and who fought for you when no one else would.

Hirsch stepped toward me, pulling me from my thoughts. "What are you thinking about?"

"Just how lucky we all are to have each other."

He nodded. "You're right. We're all very, very lucky. I'm glad we could make it."

Hirsch had extended family he celebrated with the day before, and we lucked out that he could be with us on Christmas Day.

He added, "I wouldn't miss this for the world. Though, truthfully, Audrey wouldn't stop talking about seeing Barney."

"Still haven't gotten the dog yet?"

"Not yet," Hirsch said, shaking his head. "But soon. After the holidays, we'll be on the search for our new four-legged family member."

"Your life will be forever changed."

"I have no doubt."

Before too long, the house began to fill. My mother arrived, her laughter echoing down the hall along with the scent of all the cookies we baked. My brother came in with his wife, cradling their baby. Vincent and his family followed. The living room buzzed with conversation and laughter, a mix of greetings and embraces.

Barney darted between legs, tail wagging, hoping for one of the treats my mother baked. The table groaned beneath more food and sweets than anyone could possibly finish. Cupcakes and cookies covered every platter, frosted towers of red and green that seemed to multiply each time I looked.

I stood in the center of it all, the glow of Christmas lights reflecting in the windows, the hum of joy surrounding me, and I gave thanks to God for giving me such a beautiful family. Not just the one I was born into, but the one I had found along the way. It was a very merry Christmas, indeed.

A NOTE FROM H.K. CHRISTIE

Thank you for reading *Her Silent Night*! I hope the twists kept you turning the pages late into the night.

Throughout the book, Natalie writes and reports on true crimes committed near Christmas as well as U.S. foster care statistics. Every case and statistic is real—except for the 2005 Christmas fire with the lone survivor, Robert, and of course, the crimes tied to the fictional Caleb Mercer.

If you want to dive deeper into the real cases and statistics, the sources I used in writing this book are listed below.

Oh, and one last thing: if research for this book taught me anything, it's that playing Santa and shimmying down a chimney is a *terrible* idea.

Wishing you a season of peace, joy, and maybe a few fictional scares—because real life has enough of its own.

H.K. Christie

Christmas Crimes

Adolph Laudenberg Case (1972–2003, California, USA)
"The Santa Strangler"

Adolph Theodore Laudenberg, known as "The Santa Strangler," is suspected of murdering multiple women in the early 1970s in San Pedro (Los Angeles) and San Francisco. He was convicted for the 1972 Christmas Day murder of Lois Petrie after investigators matched DNA from a coffee cup he had used to evidence from the crime scene. Although he admitted to family members that he had committed additional killings, he was charged only for the Petrie case. He was sentenced to life with the possibility of parole.

More info:

Los Angeles Times – "Man Is Charged in 1972 Murder; He Is Suspected of More Killings"

Los Angeles Times – "Man, 80, Convicted in '72 Murder"

Wikipedia – Adolph Laudenberg

Bruce McArthur Case (2010–2017, Toronto, Canada)
"Santa Claus the Serial Killer"

Between 2010 and 2017, Bruce McArthur, a landscaper in Toronto, targeted men—many from Toronto's LGBTQ "Gay Village"—often exploiting vulnerabilities such as social isolation, immigration status, or homelessness. He lured them, killed them (often by strangulation), dismembered their bodies, and hid the remains in planters and other locations. He was arrested in 2018, pleaded guilty to eight counts of first-degree murder in 2019, and was given life sentences with no parole eligibility for 25 years.

More info:

The Canadian Encyclopedia – Bruce McArthur Case

The Guardian – "'Pure Evil': Toronto Serial Killer Given Eight Life Sentences"

1992 Dayton Christmas Killings (December 24–26, 1992, Dayton, Ohio, USA)

A four-member gang known as the "Downtown Posse," with

members aged 16–20, carried out a brutal spree of robberies and murders over the Christmas holiday in 1992. Six people were killed and two others wounded. Motives included robbery and silencing potential witnesses. The ringleader, Marvallous Matthew Keene, was sentenced to death (and executed in 2009); the other three—Heather Matthews, Laura Jeanne Taylor, and DeMarcus Maurice Smith—received life sentences.

More info:

Wikipedia – 1992 Dayton Christmas Murders

Dayton Daily News – "Christmas Killings in Dayton ... Map and Timeline"

Oxygen.com – "Dayton Ohio Christmas Crime Spree, Explained"

Lawson Family Massacre (1929 – Germanton, North Carolina)

On Christmas Day 1929, Charles Lawson murdered his wife and six of their seven children before taking his own life. The surviving son, Arthur, was away on an errand.

More info:

Wikipedia – Murder of the Lawson Family

NC Department of Natural & Cultural Resources Blog

Sodder Children Disappearance (1945 – Fayetteville, West Virginia)

On Christmas Eve 1945, the Sodder family home burned down. Five children vanished and were never found, leading to decades of investigation and mystery.

More info:

Wikipedia – Sodder Children Disappearance

Smithsonian Magazine – "The Children Who Went Up in Smoke"

Denney Christmas Double Homicide (2007 – Locust Grove, Oklahoma)

Jack and Elaine Denney were found shot to death on

Christmas Day 2007. After 11 years, a tip linked Justin Walker to the murders; he pled guilty in 2019 and received a 40-year sentence.

More info:

Oxygen – "Cold Case of Neighborhood Grandparents' Christmas Slaying Solved"

News On 6 – "Tahlequah Man Pleads Guilty"

KTUL – "Decade-Old Cherokee County Double Murder Case Finally Closed"

KJRH – "Man Pleads Guilty, Gets 40 Years"

Covina Christmas Eve Massacre (2008 – Covina, California)

On Christmas Eve 2008, Bruce Jeffrey Pardo dressed as Santa Claus and attacked his ex–in-laws' home with firearms and fire, killing nine people before dying by suicide.

More info:

Wikipedia – *Covina Massacre*

Los Angeles Times – "Gunman's Careful Plans Went Awry"

ABC News – "Ninth Body Found in Christmas Eve Massacre"

Kristy Bamu Case (2010 – London, UK)

On Christmas Day 2010, Kristy Bamu, a 15-year-old visiting family in East London, was tortured and drowned by his sister Magalie Bamu and her partner Eric Bikubi, who claimed to be "purging evil." Both were convicted of murder in 2012.

More info:

The Guardian – "Witchcraft Couple Jailed for Life for Murder of Kristy Bamu"

The Independent – "Couple Guilty of Witchcraft Murder"

BBC News – "Witchcraft Murder: Boy's Death Shocks UK"

Chimney-Related Deaths

Cody Caldwell Case (2015 – Huron, California)

A 19-year-old burglary suspect climbed down a chimney during a break-in. The homeowner lit a fire, unaware anyone was inside. Caldwell died from smoke inhalation and burns.

More info: Time Magazine – "Burglar Dies After Getting Stuck in Chimney"

CBS News – "Suspected Burglar Dies in Chimney"

The Fresno Bee – "Burglar Dies in Chimney After Homeowner Lights Fire"

Harley Dilly Case (2020 – Port Clinton, Ohio)

A 14-year-old boy was found dead in a chimney after being reported missing for several weeks. Cause of death was compressive asphyxia.

More info:

Business Insider – "14-Year-Old Boy Died in Chimney: Cause Was Compressive Asphyxia"

George Brewster Case (1875 – Fulbourn, England)

An 11-year-old chimney sweep died after becoming stuck in a flue, leading to reforms in child labor laws.

More info:

Cambridge Past, Present & Future – "George Brewster: The Last Chimney Sweep Boy"

Historical Chimney Deaths (20th Century)

Multiple cases of burglars, children, and accidental deaths in chimneys throughout the 1900s.

More info:

VICE – "A Brief History of People Getting Stuck in Chimneys (and Dying)"

Phil Longcake Case (2019 – Carlisle, England)

A man became trapped at the top of a 290-foot chimney;

despite rescue efforts, he died from hypothermia and cerebral swelling.

More info:
The Guardian – "Man Dies After Being Found Dangling from Carlisle Chimney"

London Chimney Fall (2015 – London, England)
A man died after falling into a chimney shaft in London.
More info:
The Guardian – "Man Dies After Falling Down Chimney in London"

Foster Care Statistics & Programs
National Foster Care Data (United States)
Over 437,000 children live in foster care in the U.S.; only about half graduate high school on time, and fewer than 8% earn a college degree.
More info:
AFCARS Report #29 (Children's Bureau, 2022)
National Foster Youth Institute – Foster Care Facts
California Department of Education – Foster Youth Data

Programs Creating Change
- **Dec My Dorm Initiative (California):** Provides dorm essentials to foster youth transitioning to college.
- **College Bound Docket (Texas):** Connects foster youth with education, housing, and tuition waivers until age 27.
- **Missouri Family Preservation Pilot:** Funds early interventions to keep children safely in their homes.

ALSO BY H.K. CHRISTIE

The Martina Monroe Series —a nail-biting crime thriller series starring PI Martina Monroe and her unofficial partner Detective August Hirsch of the Cold Case Squad. If you like high-stakes games, jaw-dropping twists, and suspense that will keep you on the edge of your seat, then you'll love the Martina Monroe crime thriller series.

The Val Costa Series —a gripping crime thriller with heart-pounding suspense. If you love Martina, you'll love Val.

The Neighbor Two Doors Down —a dark and witty psychological thriller. If you like unpredictable twists, page-turning suspense, and unreliable narrators, then you'll love *The Neighbor Two Doors Down*.

The Selena Bailey Series (1 - 5) —a suspenseful series featuring a young Selena Bailey and her turbulent path to becoming a top-notch private investigator as led by her mentor, Martina Monroe.

A Permanent Mark A heartless killer. Weeks without answers. Can she move on when a murderer walks free? If you like riveting suspense and gripping mysteries, then you'll love *A Permanent Mark* - starring a grown up Selena Bailey.

Please Don't Go She thought she left the past behind. Until a long-buried secret pulled her back—and turned her into a killer. A fast paced and addictive revenge thriller.

∾

For H.K. Christie's full catalog go to: **www.authorhkchristie.com**

At **www.authorhkchristie.com** you can also sign up for the H.K. Christie reader club where you'll be the first to hear about upcoming novels, new releases, giveaways, promotions, and a **free e-copy of the prequel to the Martina Monroe Thriller Series, *Crashing Down*!**

ABOUT THE AUTHOR

H. K. Christie watched horror films far too early in life. Inspired by the likes of Stephen King, Jodi Picoult, true crime podcasts, and a vivid imagination she now writes suspenseful thrillers.

She found her passion for writing when she embarked on a one-woman habit breaking experiment. Although she didn't break her habit she did discover a love of writing and has been at it ever since.

When not working on her latest novel, H.K. Christie can be found eating & drinking with friends, walking around the lakes, or playing with her favorite furry pal.

She is a native and current resident of the San Francisco Bay Area.

To learn more about H.K. Christie and her books, or simply to say, "hello", go to **www.authorhkchristie.com**.

At **www.authorhkchristie.com** you can also sign up for the H.K. Christie reader club where you'll be the first to hear about upcoming novels, new releases, giveaways, promotions, and a free e-copy of the prequel to the Martina Monroe Thriller Series, *Crashing Down*!

ACKNOWLEDGMENTS

Many thanks to my Advanced Reader Team. These wonderful readers are invaluable in taking the first look at my stories and helping find typos and spreading awareness of my stories through their reviews and kind words.

To my editor Ryan Mahan thank you for all your helpful suggestions and careful edit. To my cover designer, Odile, thank you for your guidance and talent.

To my best writing buddy (aka the boss), Charlie, thank you for the looks of encouragement and reminders to take breaks. If it weren't for you, I'd be in my office all day working as opposed to catering to all of your needs and wants such as snuggles, scratches, treats, and long, meandering walks. To the mister, thank you, as always, for being by my side and encouraging me.

Last but not least, I'd like to extend a huge thank you to all of my readers. It's because of you I'm able to live the dream of being a full-time author.

Made in United States
North Haven, CT
29 November 2025